Something Shattered

Southwestern Shifters
Rescued
Relentless
Reckless
Rendered
Resilience
Reverence
Revolution
Revenge
Reluctance
Renounced
Retrograde

Southern Spirits
A Subtle Breeze
When the Dead Speak
All of the Voices
Wait util Dawn
Aftermath
What Remains
Ascension
Whirlwind

Love in Xxchange
Rory's Last Chance
Miles to Go
Bend
What Matters Most
Ex's and O's
A Bit of Me
A Bit of You
In My Arms Tonight
Where There's a Will
My Heart to Keep

Leopard's Spots
Levi
Oscar
Timothy
Isaiah
Gilbert
Esau
Sullivan
Wesley
Nischal
Justice
Sabin
Cliff

Mossy Glenn Ranch
Chaps and Hope
Ropes and Dreams
Saddles and Memories
Fences and Freedom
Riding and Regrets
Broncs and Bullies
Hay and Heartbreak
Vaqueros and Vigilance

Yes, Forever
Yes, Forever: Part One
Yes, Forever: Part Two
Yes, Forever: Part Three
Yes, Forever: Part Four
Yes, Forever: Part Five

Spotless
Hide
Hunt
Home
Heart

Coyote's Call
Off Course
In from the Cold

Coyote's Call

BLUE MOON RISING

BAILEY BRADFORD

Blue Moon Rising
ISBN # 978-1-78651-857-6
©Copyright Bailey Bradford 2016
Cover Art by Posh Gosh ©Copyright February 2016
Interior text design by Claire Siemaszkiewicz
Pride Publishing

Published in 2016 by Pride Publishing, Newland House, The Point, Weaver Road, Lincoln, LN6 3QN, United Kingdom.

BLUE MOON RISING

Dedication

To the people who've supported me and who accept
and understand my silences. Thank you.

Chapter One

Pain. It was the one constant in Abraham Evans' life. Despite the medication to counter it that was dripping into his veins via an IV, pain followed him into sleep. His chest and back burned with it—a hot, coiling agony that seemed to never ebb much. If he could have, he'd have just drifted away and never come back to his body.

He'd seen himself lying there on the hospital bed a couple of times. The first instance, he'd flipped out, panicked, tried to scream and make himself move as doctors and nurses rushed around him. When he'd slammed back into that traitorous body, agony unlike anything Abraham had ever felt had scorched every one of his nerves.

The second time, he'd been less scared, and more worried that he'd be pulled back into his body. Which he had been, by the dedicated staff at St. Luke's Hospital.

Abraham knew where he was, had a sort of cognizance about what had happened to him. He'd been poisoned and shot, and he'd died—three times since. None of the dying had stuck, but the pain clung to him like a multi-tentacled demon unwilling to give him respite.

The third time he'd died, Abraham had fought against being pulled down into his body again. That body had betrayed him, was weak and giving up on his soul or whatever floaty part of him was out of it.

Abraham had worked all his life to be strong, to be virtually bulletproof. He wasn't supposed to be taken out so easily. His body was supposed to be closer to invincible, or at least not so weak.

Yet there he was, hooked up to more machines than any living person ought to be without being half robot. The *beeps* and *swishes* they made kept him from truly resting. He heard them, just as he heard the doctors and nurses, and the few visitors he had, even when those people said he was in a coma.

And sometimes, he left his body while the medical equipment still worked, and he looked around the hospital room, at his coworkers, fellow Texas Rangers, who were checking in on him, or at Miller Hudson and his partner, Gideon Wells.

But Abraham didn't see the one person he longed for. He thought maybe that was why he didn't want to wake up.

He didn't have any business longing for the young man who never visited. There was no reason for him to feel abandoned by him or hurt. Abraham wasn't sure those were issues he was experiencing anyway. All he really was in touch with was that he hurt, so bad, and he was tired of hurting. If dying meant the pain ended, he was ready for his life to end.

Yet it didn't. *He* didn't. Instead, the machines droned and chirped, and medical staff came in to examine Abraham. Visitors showed up, though not too often now that he'd been in the hospital for a while. Abraham didn't know the passing of the days and nights, but it felt like he'd been there in that bed for a long time.

He was tired, and ready for things to change. He just needed to decide *what* kind of change he wanted to occur—either he willed himself dead and gone, or he focused on trying to get better.

It wasn't as easy a choice to make as Abraham would have once believed it to be.

* * * *

Opening his eyes almost took more effort than it was worth. Abraham wasn't sure he'd even managed it until someone congratulated him on coming back to the world. His vision was so blurry, at first Abraham feared he'd damaged his eyes permanently, but some frantic blinking made a minimal difference.

"Here. You've got ointment in your eyes. Don't get scared when I press this cloth to them."

Abraham didn't recognize the speaker. Her voice was steady and sure, though, so he was inclined to trust that she knew what she was doing. After she'd finished her ministrations, Abraham's eyes began to focus.

"Well, it's so good you decided to come back to us," she said. "We took your tube out and have been slowly wakening you."

Scrubs -- nurse. Abraham's brain made the connection. She had short gray hair and a round, pleasant face. Her smile held kindness, or it seemed so to him. Regardless, Abraham didn't smile back.

"I'm Barb, and I'm on shift until eleven tonight." Barb glanced away. "Oh, and here's Doctor Molina, coming to check you over."

More poking and prodding, just what Abraham wanted. But, he'd decided to put every effort he could into getting better. He was still furious at his body for being so weak and failing him, but there were things still tying him to his life. Something inside him had awakened and pushed him not to give up. Even now, he felt it, pulsing with determination, like an echo of his heartbeat.

Whatever it was, Abraham was too tired to fight it. *Funny that means staying alive.*

"Ranger Evans, so good to see you awake and alert today," said a man who had to be Dr. Molina, since that was how Barb had addressed him. "You have given us quite a few scares, but that's in the past now, isn't it? You're going to pull through this."

Abraham managed a grunt. His throat ached and confusion was swamping him.

"You're going to be just fine now, Ranger Evans," Dr. Molina was saying as he bent over Abraham. "You're healing well from the last surgery, and your vitals are stronger than they've been in a while. All in all, you're finally recovering."

Abraham had vague memories of surgeries along with his experiences with death. What he didn't have was a concept of time. "How long?" he tried to ask, but merely croaked.

"Ice chips," Dr. Molina said over his shoulder. "Let me check your incision then I'll answer your question."

It was tempting to close his eyes again, but now that Abraham was awake, he was kind of afraid to. He'd decided to fight, to live. *What if I close my eyes, fall asleep, and that's it…I'm just…gone?*

"It looks very good, very good." Dr. Molina straightened up. "Now, mouth what you asked. Your voice isn't going to work so well, and you are very disoriented. You've been sedated for several days and it takes over seventy-two hours sometimes for people who've been in your situation to be able to articulate a coherent thought."

Abraham didn't feel incoherent, or confused. He didn't feel like he was unaware of himself, or the situation. That thing inside him was pulsing, telling him he needed to get up and get better. "How long?" he mouthed just before a nurse slipped an ice chip past his lips.

"Total?" Dr. Molina didn't wait for him to nod or reply. "Over a month. As I said, you've given us quite a few scares, Ranger Evans, but you are very resilient and you were in such good shape—before you were shot and poisoned—that your body didn't give up easily. Not many people would have survived what you have made it through."

Abraham didn't miss the past tense usage about him having been in good shape. Over a month of being laid up in a hospital bed, most of it with him unconscious, meant he was weak and pathetic, and had probably lost a lot of muscle mass.

"You'll be regaining your strength in no time," Dr. Molina continued. "Tomorrow, we'll try getting you up, to sit, at least, if not to stand. Physical therapy will begin the day after. Do what you're told, and don't bark at the PTs too much, okay? Now let me just have a look at your eyes and throat."

Like I could stop you? Abraham wasn't even sure he could lift his hands. Holding his eyelids open was tiring him out.

Dr. Molina finished his exam, then patted Abraham's foot and gave him a distracted smile. "You'll be out of here in no time, Ranger Evans." He smiled and left the room.

"Your friends and fellow Rangers will be so glad to see you awake," Barb said, tucking his sheet around his legs. "Would you like me to contact anyone for you?"

Abraham hated the idea of anyone seeing him like he was, though he'd looked worse before he'd come to consciousness, he supposed. Even so, he wasn't eager for company. He gave the smallest shake of his head.

Barb nodded. "Okay, but this is the day you usually have a couple of visitors. Your parents, I believe, if what Mindy told me was right, and your friends—not the Ranger ones. The regular citizen ones." Barb smiled brightly. "Mindy's been your nurse for this shift since you came in here, but she had to take off for personal reasons, so you get to have me here instead."

Abraham was stuck on hearing that his parents visited him regularly. He had no recollection of them being there, no memories of their voices as he lay in a coma, whereas he did remember other people.

And maybe that meant he'd hallucinated it all—the voices he'd heard, him dying, the making a choice to live. That seemed more likely than his parents coming to visit him under any circumstance.

Chapter Two

There was something in the air, a warning carried on the breeze as it tickled the hair on Roman Jonas' forearms. He looked up, alarm streaking down his spine. Standing outside the ceremonial hall his pack used, Roman was well aware that there were enemies still on the loose — mad men, cat shifters — who'd tried to kill him and his friends. He was never not aware of that, had carried the stress of it since being attacked and assaulted as a young teenage boy.

That he couldn't remember all of the assault was a blessing and a curse. Roman couldn't help but feel that if he remembered everything, he would be able to heal completely. At the very least, he'd know just how many men had hurt him, and how.

His gut cramped and he winced. Maybe he didn't want to know those things after all.

Roman sniffed, but nothing unfamiliar came to him on the wind. He smelled desert and adobe, cactus and just a hint of pine. Nothing living that was a danger to him. Trusting his senses might not be the smart thing to do, however. It wasn't like he could shift into his coyote form yet. Almost everyone else in the pack had gained that ability. It seemed shameful of him, as their medicine man in training, to not be able to do so.

Miller, his alpha, told Roman to give it time.

Roman sighed and brushed back the hair from his bangs. They'd grown out, and kept flopping in his eyes.

After another moment of standing still and trying to sense if there was danger near after all, Roman finally had to believe he was safe enough. Miller had people nearby, keeping an eye out for trouble. Roman hadn't been left unguarded since the attack that had occurred over a month ago at the ceremonial hall.

"I'm okay," he murmured to himself. His heart fluttered oddly, and Roman wondered if he was about to pass out or if his heart had something wrong with it. He'd had panic and anxiety attacks, and both made him feel like he was having a heart attack. This was different, almost as if some helium had seeped into his chest.

Roman mentally rolled his eyes at himself and knelt in front of the newly built garden. He had better things to do than to stand around worrying if he was about to die.

The ground was hard beneath his knees, but the sectioned off garden that ran the length of the ceremony hall on either side of the small porch was going to look gorgeous once his plants bloomed. But first, Roman had to get his ass in gear and actually put those plants in the ground.

The Texas desert wasn't the best place to try to grow anything. The garden, however, had excellent soil mixed into it and was raised a few inches off the ground for drainage. Roman had read up on raised box gardening before starting this venture. He had plants in the nursery, too, though less after the fighting that had taken place in there.

Well, now he was going to have some more.

Roman dug his hands into the soil and felt a contentment that was all too rare for him. He felt at home when he was gardening, as if he were doing something important and useful. It relaxed him and pleased him as well.

He held his hands up, cupping dirt in them, then slowly turned his hands and let the soil fall back down. "We're going to grow something beautiful here, you and I," he promised it.

The sun beat down on him as Roman worked, digging holes, sliding the plants into them, tucking their roots in safe and gently. Sweat drenched him, but Roman didn't care if he was soaking wet or if he smelled ripe. The peace it gave him to work as he was doing was worth any price.

His knees ached after a while, but Roman ignored the pain, intent on getting every plant he'd chosen into the ground. No one bothered him, which was nice. Roman liked being alone more and more. Solitude offered him respite from the pressures of being a medicine man. Meditation had become one of his favorite things.

Even so, there was always a little piece of him that wasn't satisfied. He couldn't pinpoint why that was, what that was — Roman only knew it was there, in him. Something was missing besides his coyote form.

Once he had finished with the garden, Roman stood up and stretched, groaning a little at the aches and pains that came along with kneeling and hunching over for hours. He wiggled a little, arms overhead, trying to shake out some of the stiffness in his body, then he lowered his arms and dusted off his knees. "Maybe I should get some of those gardening knee pads." He'd seen them on TV before. Roman gingerly touched his knees. "Ow." Definitely tender, but he'd survive.

He took a moment to survey his hard work, then turned as he heard an engine off in the distance. Roman recognized the sound of it—Miller, and likely Miller's mate, Gideon, were coming up the road leading to the center.

Roman shielded his eyes with one hand and watched until he saw the truck round the curve. Assured he was right about the visitors' identity, he trotted into the building, shivering as the cold air from the AC hit his heated skin.

Roman hurried to the bathroom and peeled off his stinky clothes. He noted his red face and groaned. He'd forgotten sunscreen, or a hat, and his pale skin was going to make him pay for that. He'd blister and peel and look like a gross mess for a week.

"Well, maybe I'll remember next time." Roman stuck his tongue out at his reflection then stepped into the shower. He turned the spigots on, halfway for both, and the first chilly burst of water made him yelp before the hot and cold reached a nice, lukewarm temperature.

Even that felt too hot for his face and his arms. Roman guessed he was lucky he'd been kneeling and his legs weren't burnt, too.

He bathed quickly, scrubbing off the sweat and dirt, even cleaning out from under his fingernails. When he felt like he'd gotten himself spick and span, Roman shut the shower off then got out and dried with his favorite towel.

He brushed his teeth and put on deodorant and, with the towel around his hips, headed out of the bathroom, into his bedroom. He knew Miller and Gideon would be waiting for him in the nursery, which was also

Roman's office. He felt more at peace around the plants than anywhere else.

He dressed in a pair of soft cotton pants and a blousy, almost sheer white shirt. His nipples showed through the material but Roman didn't worry about it. Neither Miller nor Gideon would think he was trying to catch their attention. The shirt was just soft and sensual, and Roman loved the way it felt on his skin.

He brushed his long white-blond hair and tucked it up into the much-maligned man-bun. He didn't do it to be hip or to fit in. His hair was growing out and it was hot, and Roman wanted it off his nape and back.

Barefoot, he left his bedroom and traipsed to the nursery, finding comfort in the gold pine planks that made up the walls of the interior of the building. Paintings, blankets and nature-inspired art decorated the walls and shelves. Roman picked up the last two bowls he'd finished making the night before, having placed them on the hall stand, and took them with him so he could give them to Miller.

The mesquite wood bowls sold quickly, and for a good price. Roman enjoyed making them, and the money he earned helped him feel like a contributing member of society rather than a damaged boy.

I'm a man, not a boy. I haven't been a kid for a while now.

He stepped into the nursery and was greeted by his alpha and Gideon, both of whom appeared to be very happy about something, judging by their broad smiles. Until they looked at him.

"Roman, you know you burn like that." Miller snapped his fingers. "You're going to be miserable tomorrow."

Roman ducked his head. "I'll put aloe vera on it in a few minutes." Which is what he should have done in the first place, because it might prevent him from blistering and peeling. Or at least blistering.

"Make sure that you do," Miller advised.

"I will." Roman raised his head and held out his hands.

"More bowls? Great!" Gideon held out his hands. "These will be gone before I can even put them out in the gallery. I've had seven people email me and ask for one of Roman Jonas' mesquite bowls." He set them carefully on the small desk tucked across from the first row of plants. "I made a deposit into your PayPal account today, too."

"Thank you." Roman would check that later.

"The garden out front looks amazing," Miller said, leaning one hip against the desk and folding his arms over his chest. "The shade should help keep the plants from frying under the sun."

"Yes, and thank you again for that." Roman had merely mentioned the possibility of installing retractable awnings across the front of the building, and Miller had taken over from there. Roman had had his awnings in less than a week. "I really like the green color."

"We need more green out here." Miller smiled as Gideon moved to stand beside him. "So, I wanted to let you know that Abraham—Ranger Evans—woke up. Well, he isn't going to be a Ranger any longer, but he's alive, and improving."

Guilt curled in Roman's stomach, a hot, vile ball that felt like it weighed a ton. "Th-that's good." He couldn't quite look at Miller or Gideon. "I'm glad he didn't die."

"Yeah, me too. He's had a rough go of it, and I guess, like I mentioned, he won't be a Ranger anymore. The damage to his right shoulder and arm is pretty severe."

Roman glanced at Miller then. "How severe?"

"Well, he didn't lose his arm, but from what I understand, he'll be lucky if he can make a fist, and he can't raise his arm above about here." Miller held his right hand up, about ten inches above his waist. "He was pretty upset about that, according to his dad, and ain't *that* man a barrel of fun. Jesus. Talk about having a stick up your ass—that phrase was made just for Mr. Evans and his uptight wife."

"I don't think Abraham likes his parents being there, but I could be wrong. He's so stoic, I can't really tell what he likes and doesn't like." Gideon muttered the last bit. "If you want to go see him-"

"No," Roman said sharply, more so than he'd intended. He looked away from Gideon and Miller. "No, I can't."

"Can't?" Miller asked. "Ro, what's going on?"

Roman swiped a hand over his mouth, as if he could encourage the right words out of it. But the truth was, he didn't have an answer. Ranger Evans—*Abraham*—made him feel strange inside, and dealing with that was too much for Roman, at least it was at this point in his life.

"It's okay. You don't have to tell us anything. Just, you know we're here for you."

Roman nodded. "Yeah. Thanks for that, Miller."

"As far as I've heard, there's no new information on the Vonheimers that escaped. Pisses me off. I'd like this to be over, and them to be done with," Miller said.

He sounded angry, which was unusual. Miller was generally laid-back. But the Vonheimers had done unspeakable things to Roman, and had tried to kill him as well as several other pack members.

And they'd very nearly killed Abraham Evans. That thought caused a pinching in Roman's chest that he couldn't rub away, though he tried.

"You okay? Something wrong?" Miller was suddenly beside him.

Roman hadn't even heard him move. "I'm fine. Just... Just tired, I guess. Frustrated. I want those people out of my life forever, and I want to be able to shift. What kind of medicine man can I be for this pack if I can't even shift? No one will follow my advice much longer if I'm locked in human form."

Miller tucked a finger under Roman's chin and tipped his head up. "Can you feel your coyote?"

"Can *you* feel him in me?" Roman countered, because he barely felt anything of it at all.

Miller peered into his eyes unblinkingly. Roman tried to do the same, but it was hard to meet his alpha's direct stare like that. He blinked more than once.

Miller rumbled, the sound coming from deep in his chest, not a human noise at all.

That wild coyote inside Miller was calling out to Roman's hidden one, but all Roman felt was a twitch in his core, like he'd swallowed a flea and it'd bounced around — just a tiny sensation.

"He's there," Miller said, without a hint of doubt. "He's not ready to come out yet. Roman, I think..." Miller moved his finger, letting Roman lower his chin. "I think maybe what happened in the past is restricting your coyote still."

"Great," Roman snapped. "So I have to move past being...being..." He couldn't say it, not what had really happened. "Hurt, before I can shift? That's messed up. Like I'm still the mess I was back then, and I'm not."

"I could be wrong." Miller shrugged. "Look, I didn't shift until I was a lot older than you, you know that. Don't stress yourself out over this, not yet at least."

Roman didn't argue or agree. He felt petulant and more like his former, moody self than he had in months. What he didn't feel like was a mature adult, much less one that was going to be responsible for his entire pack's spiritual needs, at the very least. The weight of that was becoming more of a burden than a blessing some days.

And Roman was ashamed of feeling that way. He didn't want to let Miller or the pack down. He knew, too, that he was supposed to be where he was, doing what he was. Just…sometimes it was hard not to buck and bow out, not to run and leave all his responsibilities behind.

Not that he'd ever run away. Roman had a secret he shared with no one—he was terrified of the idea of being alone, as in, on his own without a family or pack. He'd *never* leave them.

"You're pretty lost in whatever thoughts you've got going on, Ro. Are you sure you're okay?" Miller asked.

Roman tried to smile reassuringly and hoped he succeeded. "I'm fine. Just thinking about some research I need to do."

"Oh!" Gideon bounded over, exciting all but bubbling out of him. "I forgot to tell you, I found this *amazing* book on shamanism, it's four hundred years old and is considered a sacred text—we're not discussing how I found it—but it'll be here tomorrow. I know it has to be handled carefully and all, but the lady bringing it to me said she'd explain everything we needed to know about it. Maybe you can learn more stuff from the book."

"As long as she ain't scammin' us," Miller groused.

"If she is, I can eat her," Gideon joked, smacking his lips together afterwards.

Miller wrinkled his nose at his mate. "Gross, Gid."

Gideon giggled and slipped an arm around Miller. "You know I'm only interested in nibbling on you, sweet stuff."

"Better be," Miller said to Gideon before looking at Roman. "When you finish up here, come to the house. The Fervent Five will be here to pick you up. We're having Mom's homemade organic pizzas tonight."

"I'll be there," Roman promised, his mouth already watering. Jess Hudson's pizzas were not to be missed. Though she usually only made them for special occasions. "What're we celebrating?"

Miller and Gideon exchanged a glance that had Roman's imaginary hackles rising.

"What is it?" he demanded.

Miller answered, "Mom and Jack are tying the knot next month in the town square, and... Well, it's not really about... But I guess it is—"

"Jeez, Miller, just say it," Gideon urged. "Or I will. Yeah, I will. We invited Abraham to move here, into the apartments we set up. He's going to need all the help he can get, and he doesn't seem to want his folks bothering him. Iker and Gael will be around to assist him with anything he needs, and get him to his PT sessions in El Paso. But... I guess Miller figured you wouldn't think having Abraham here is something to celebrate, and anyway, it isn't like Abraham has said yes yet. We're just hoping he does. Though, if that's going to really be a problem for you, I guess we could rescind the offer."

"No, don't do that. It's fine. I'm fine." Roman didn't know why Abraham Evans affected him like he did, but there was zero chance of Roman denying the man the help it sounded like he needed. Besides, Roman stayed at the ceremonial hall for the most part. He never went to the new apartments Miller and Gideon had built for shifters in need of homes and, apparently, humans in need of help.

The internal buzz of excitement didn't surprise Roman. There was something about Abraham Evans that did funny things to him. At first he'd been scared by his reaction to the man.

Now he wasn't sure what, exactly, he felt for Evans, but fear wasn't the predominant emotion in the mix — if it was even there at all.

Chapter Three

"No." Abraham didn't so much as dither. "I am *not* being released into your care."

His mother pursed her lips but other than that, showed no signs of irritation.

"You most certainly are," his father boomed. "You can't get yourself to and from physical therapy and you need assistance."

Abraham gestured to Barb, who looked like she wanted to say a few choice words to his parents. "No, and *yes*, I can get myself to and from therapy. I may not be up to driving but I can damn well call for a taxi."

His father looked flabbergasted. "Taxis? That's ridiculous! Why would you bother when you could hire a driver? You aren't of sound mind, and—"

"He most certainly is of sound mind," Barb interrupted. "Don't even try that kind of bull here. I, along with everyone who has been involved in Mr. Evans' care, will vouch for the soundness of his mind, as well as for your refusal to leave when he's asked you to. He could have banned you both from coming up here, but he didn't. I suggest you leave him alone as he's requested, now, before security is called."

"I'll be filing a complaint against you," his father warned, pointing at Barb.

Barb grinned and held the door open for them. "You do that."

Once his parents had left, Barb's smile slipped away. "What *is* their problem? They come up every few days or so, sit in your room for one hour, and don't even speak to you beyond saying 'hello, son'. Then they expect you to go home with them?"

"It's all about the money," Abraham admitted. He liked Barb—she'd been kind to him when he needed it, and assertive when he'd needed his ass kicked into gear, but she'd never been cruel or short with him. "I'm wealthy. They aren't. At least not like I am. My grandmother left them enough to be comfortable when she passed away, but left the bulk of her wealth to me." It wasn't something he normally shared. Abraham was going to blame his loose tongue on the pain meds making him stoned, and Barb's acute ability to listen like she cared. He supposed she did. She really was very nice.

"Money?" Barb laughed, rolling her eyes a bit. "Figures. It's always about money or sex. Ew, though not sex with parents, that's just wrong on so many levels. Sorry if it sounded like I approved."

"I don't usually tell anyone that, about me. The money, I mean," Abraham said, trying to order his thoughts and mouth to work together. "You're very trustworthy."

Barb laughed again. "Oh, it's just that I've been here helping and, well, I'm irresistible." She batted her lashes at him. "Just ask my husband. He says he knew he was going to marry me after our first date. I took a little more convincing than that, but…he *is* my soul mate. Everybody has one, you know."

Abraham saw no need to tell her his soul mate might not exist. She seemed so certain and happy.

"Now, your friends will be here in a little while to get you. What in the world makes you want to go stay in a dinky town like Del Rey?" Barb waved off her own question. "Those friends, of course. They are upstanding guys. I'm glad they can marry now. Are they going to?"

"Dunno. I haven't asked them." Abraham hadn't thought to. He'd been preoccupied with his own pain and suffering.

"They should. You can tell by looking at them that they're made for each other." Barb sat down in the chair beside the bed. "I'm actually off today, remember? Had a feeling your parents would be, hmm, pushy."

It was only then Abraham realized Barb was wearing jeans and a T-shirt instead of scrubs. "Oh, you didn't have to do that. Come in on your day off. I mean."

"I didn't mind, and besides, Malachi, my husband, is out of town on a run. He drives a big rig, and usually he's got his schedule set up so we're home together, but that's not always possible, so, here I am. I want to check up on Mrs. Daniels and Mr. Johnson, too. I'm really worried about them."

Abraham knew they were elderly patients that Barb had grown attached to, or perhaps had known before they'd become ill. He wasn't clear on that part of it, just that Barb had a lot of compassion for her patients. "They're lucky to have you, and so was I."

"Well, if you need help, or you feel like meeting for lunch one of the days you have therapy in town, let me know." Barb got up and gave him a quick hug. "I think I hear your friends coming."

Abraham had given up knowing how Barb could tell him someone was on the way to the room before he ever heard a peep out of them. She was never wrong, however.

She crossed over to the door then opened it, smiling and waving at someone outside. Sure enough, less than twenty seconds later, Miller and Gideon came into the room.

Gideon gave him two thumbs up. "The nurse at the front desk said you'll be out of here in just a few more minutes. He sent someone for a wheelchair."

As much as Abraham wanted to protest that he could walk out on his own, he knew the rule was that he had to be wheeled out. And he wasn't too sure how far he could walk. He was as weak as could be, not that he wanted to admit to such.

"Here you go, and Dr. Molina is coming by— Oh, here's the man himself!" The male nurse currently in the room wasn't one Abraham had met before, but he seemed chirpy and entirely too happy to see Dr. Molina.

Dr. Molina's cheeks turned a dusky brown. "JJ, did you have an extra cup of coffee this morning?"

"More like an extra pot of it," Barb said, smiling at the male nurse. "And a dozen donuts."

"God, I had these chocolate filled ones that were *so* good!"

Abraham turned his attention from the nurses to the doctor. "Am I free now?"

Dr. Molina handed him his discharge papers. "You are. Make sure you and whoever is helping you reads through these. Note the appointment times you have. I've got you scheduled for a check-up with me next Friday at my office about three blocks down from the hospital. Don't skip out on therapy, and remember, you still have mobility in your right arm and hand."

"Just not much," Abraham said. "Not enough to grip a gun." His career was over. All he'd ever wanted was to be a Texas Ranger, and now he was going to have to consider a new path in life.

"You're alive, and overall, whole. Be thankful for that." Dr. Molina patted his shoulder — Molina seemed to be the touchy-feely sort. "I thought for certain we'd lost you a couple of times. Now, go out and do what it takes to be as strong as you can. But don't push too hard. It won't do you any good if you hurt yourself trying to get better quicker."

"Yeah, I already had that lecture at the PT center here." Abraham held his left hand out awkwardly to Dr. Molina. "Thank you."

"You're very welcome." Molina's grip was firm but not painfully so. "Miller, Gideon, if you have any questions, feel free to call. Same goes for you, Mr. Evans."

For some reason, Molina was on a first name basis with everyone but him. If that should have bothered Abraham, it didn't. "Thanks, Dr. Molina."

Abraham got from the bed to the wheelchair on his own, but falling was a near thing. He detested the weakness that ruled him now. *I'm not going to wallow in self-pity. I'm alive. That's what counts, that, and Roman wasn't hurt, is still safe.* He hadn't asked about Roman, but almost every visit, Miller had mentioned the young man who'd had such a horrific crime committed against him years ago.

It wasn't right for Abraham to want Roman like he did, so he kept that want buried. One, he had to be close to fifteen years older than Roman, and two, he'd seen the pictures of what had been done to him. Abraham didn't know if anyone could get past that kind of trauma. As far as he knew, Roman didn't have intimate relations with anyone, not that Abraham spied on him or anything. It was just from things he heard. Miller and Gideon never mentioned Roman in conjunction with a possible date, boyfriend, or girlfriend.

"Bet you're glad to be sprung of that place," Miller said as he pushed the wheelchair toward the automatic doors after they'd gotten out of the hospital room. "You gave that nurse your number. You sweet on her?"

Abraham would have laughed at that, had he had it in him. "Nope. She's happily married, but she might be a friend. I think she is." Honestly, he hadn't had enough of them to know for sure.

Gideon made a *hmm* sort of noise. "Well, that's nice of her, then, as long as she isn't trying to hit it up with you behind her husband's back."

That comment pissed Abraham off, though he tried to keep from snapping too much. "Why would you even say that? Is every guy that you talk to or count as a friend trying to get in your pants?"

"Not if he wants to keep his balls," Miller snarled. "And I don't mean Gid. I *know* Gid's mine, and I'm his. Doesn't mean other idiots don't always understand that, or see it as a challenge."

"Okay, so in the same way that you can have male friends, I can have female friends." *Or female friend. There's just Barb...and I think Miller and Gideon are my friends, too.* It was a sudden, and likely ridiculous, realization. If Miller and Gideon weren't his friends, why had they visited so often and offered him a place to stay, as well as help getting to his appointments and whatever else he needed done?

An odd, subtle warmth began to work its way out from his chest. Not a painful sensation, but one that

Abraham recognized as happiness. He hadn't felt anything like it in so long that he almost gasped, but not wanting to appear to be a weirdo, he pressed his lips tightly together instead and remained quiet.

He didn't have to speak, anyway, because Gideon chattered non-stop on the way to the truck. And while helping Abraham into the truck. And while getting in himself. And for the entire drive to Del Rey.

It should have annoyed Abraham, yet he found himself relaxing and even enjoying Gideon's babbling. It wasn't all directed to him, anyway. Miller got an earful about what kind of changes Gideon wanted to make to the gallery, the difference between ecru and ivory, the difference being one had a little more of a yellow tinge to it.

Abraham filed that away with useless knowledge he'd never need, but that would occupy a space his brain should be using for more important shit.

He ended up dozing off and on, daring to break the law and unbuckle his seat belt so he could lie down in the back seat. Sitting upright hurt, slouching hurt— he'd risk not wearing the seat belt if it meant escaping some of the hellish level of pain.

Eventually, he felt the truck slowing down, and Abraham cautiously sat up, taking his time to do so. He saw that they had just hit the town limits of Del Rey, and tried not to let out a sigh of relief. He wanted to get to where he was going, and go to sleep for a dozen hours. He'd been poked and prodded and woken up entirely too much in the hospital.

"Can I stop by the gallery real quick, or do I need to get you home first?" Miller asked. "I just need to check on Roman and the Fervent Five."

Gideon twisted around to peer at Abraham. "The Double F's being Tandy, Paul, Brandt, Frisky and Kyra.

They like to hang around wherever Roman's at to make sure he's safe. I think it makes him, and them, all feel better."

At the mention of Roman's name, any objection to stopping Abraham had died on his tongue. He dipped his head, a quick nod, and swiped at his mouth in case he'd drooled any while he'd dozed.

Though he doubted Roman would come outside to see him, anyway. Roman had never once come to the hospital, which hadn't been a surprise. He wasn't a friend, or even an acquaintance. He'd been a victim of a crime Abraham had been hoping to solve.

But now Abraham was no longer a Ranger, and he wasn't restricted by his vow to serve and protect first, though he still would. He could ask Roman out, which was something he wouldn't have been able to do before he'd had to step down as a Ranger. Maybe it wouldn't have been against the rules, exactly, had he asked Roman out before, but it would have gotten Abraham yanked from his case.

And now he wasn't on any case. That didn't mean he'd ask Roman out.

What he would do, was what he'd been trying to do before being hurt. He'd do his best to make sure Roman was safe, and to bring his attackers to justice.

Miller pulled the truck up to the curb in front of the gallery. "I'll be right back."

"Hey, I'm coming with you." Gideon glanced back at Abraham again. "If that's okay?"

"Go on." Abraham was perfectly capable of sitting by himself in the truck.

Although, when Roman appeared in the doorway of the gallery, and immediately looked right at him, Abraham thought he was having a heart attack. He even tried to clutch at his chest until his right arm protested and pain exploded bright and hot in his shoulder. Black and white dots danced before his eyes. There was a roaring in his ears, though it only lasted for a second or two. The opening of the truck door snapped Abraham back into himself, out of the haze of pain he'd tumbled into.

"Hey, are you okay, Ranger, um, Evans?"

Abraham opened his eyes, unaware that he'd ever closed them, and felt a little dizzy when he found himself looking right into Roman Jonas' pretty green and brown eyes. "Hazel."

Roman blinked. "I'm sorry? I should…sh-should get someone —"

"No, no I'm fine," Abraham got past his stupid lips. "Just woke up, is all. I was a little confused for a minute there."

"Oh." Roman gulped, the sound loud in the cab of the truck.

Abraham realized that Roman had climbed almost all the way into the cab, with one knee planted on the floor board. There should have been something else for Abraham to say, but all he could do was sit and stare.

Roman was a very pretty man, with fine, delicate features except for his large, hazel eyes. His nose was pert and perfectly straight, his mouth lush and pink. His fine, white-blond hair hung past his shoulders, and looked soft as silk. For some reason, Roman had captivated his attention since the first time they'd met, and Abraham had quit trying to figure out why.

"I wanted to come say th-thank you," Roman said a moment later, averting his gaze. "I should have come to visit you at the hospital, but I didn't know if that would be weird."

"No, it was fine. Don't be sorry about that." Abraham didn't want Roman feeling bad about anything. "I didn't like anyone seeing me all busted up. Still can't walk more than a few feet before I'm worn out." Admitting his weakness made his cheeks burn with shame. He didn't know why he'd done it, unless part of him knew that Roman needed to hear it, to know that Abraham wasn't a threat. That he wasn't always the strong one.

Before he could figure out what to say next, Miller and Gideon came outside with four young adults following them. A fifth one, a perky-looking guy, all but bounced out after them. "Wait up!"

Whatever intimate moment had been building between Abraham and Roman snapped like a wire stretched too far.

"Oh, I— It was good to see you." Roman ducked his head and moved away from the truck.

Abraham was left stunned. He thought that was the most Roman had ever said to him, and the semi-spooked look he usually saw in Roman's eyes had been missing. Then again, it was possible Abraham had just missed it. He still felt a little stoned from the patchy sleep he'd gotten.

"Hi, Ranger Evans—er." One of the men, a bouncy brunet, blushed darkly.

Abraham remembered seeing the young people gathered around the open door before, but names were escaping him just then.

"Way to go, Brandt," a woman muttered. "Just stick your foot right in your mouth."

"Tandy, leave him alone," Miller said, touching the man's—*Brandt's*—arm while looking at Abraham. "This is Brandt, that's Tandy, Kyra, Frisky and Paul." Miller pointed out each person as he said their name. "Also known as the Fervent Five."

"Because when we make up our mind about something, there's no turning back," Tandy added.

Abraham thought that might be the creepiest thing, ever. Like the five of them were really one being, sharing a single brain.

Brandt moved to the open door. "Sorry about the Ranger thing. I didn't mean anything by it. But isn't it kinda like the Marines? You know, once a Marine, always a Marine, there's no such thing as an ex-Marine?"

"You really should have not started talking again," Kyra said as she nudged Brandt aside. "He doesn't mean to be annoying. Usually. Sometimes. Maybe."

"That's enough, y'all. Let us get Abraham to his apartment." Miller and Gideon shooed everyone away.

Abraham noted that Roman was already back inside the gallery by then, not lingering around like he'd wanted to talk again. That didn't mean anything, wasn't a reason to feel rebuffed or hurt. Abraham closed his eyes. He was so tired, and over being easily exhausted, but there was nothing he could do about it now. It was easier to let sleep take him out of his worries, so Abraham dozed until they arrived at the apartments.

He rubbed his eyes upon awakening.

"Yeah, here we are. We don't have many people living here yet, but that's okay. There's Duff, Gael and Iker for now. And you. You have the middle apartment on the bottom floor." Miller shut the truck off and unbuckled his seat belt.

Abraham had never put his back on. He opened his door, then carefully eased himself out of the truck.

"Here, let me help." Gideon was at his left side before Abraham's feet hit the ground. "You don't have to play the silent, macho part with me. Not that you aren't macho. Or silent. I'll just shut up now."

Miller snickered. Abraham didn't have the energy to so much as grunt. He let Gideon help him into the apartment, barely noticing the exterior of the place. Inside, the small efficiency was decorated and furnished. All of Abraham's belongings were, for the most part, still at his apartment in El Paso.

He wasn't going to examine why he'd let himself be talked — easily — into coming to Del Rey. Not yet, and maybe not ever.

Abraham had just followed his instincts, and they'd told him to agree when Miller had offered him the apartment and any help. As he looked around his new, temporary home, Abraham realized it probably suited him more than where he'd been living before. Here, there were framed paintings on the wall, and knick-knacks on the end tables and shelves.

"I hope this is okay," Miller was saying. "Nothing fancy, but just about everyone pitched in to make it cozy for you. Mom made you several meals, they're in the fridge and freezer, with labels and directions and all that kinda stuff. We've got a schedule for you letting you know who's coming by and when, who's taking you to your appointments and phone numbers — all that's on the fridge, right there under the magnet."

Abraham glanced at the refrigerator. "Thank you." His throat was tight, clogged with emotion and gratitude. He couldn't remember the last time someone had done him so much kindness.

"You want to relax on the couch or go right to bed?" Gideon asked, still helping him stay upright. "I bet it's time for more pain meds, too."

"Bed, please," Abraham rasped. He needed to get his emotions under control, because he was awfully close to doing something embarrassing, like crying.

"Sure thing." Gideon helped him over to the bed, then assisted Abraham in lying down. "There's a can right here." Gideon tapped the wooden handle. The can was between the bed and the nightstand. "Cell phone will be right here, too. I'll be back with your medicine and some water."

Abraham was vaguely aware of taking some pills and washing them down with cold water. Someone took the glass from him as his eyelids grew too heavy to keep open, and he finally drifted off to sleep.

Chapter Four

Roman couldn't shake the image of Ranger Evans hunched in the back seat of the truck, looking like he'd met Death, and shook his hand. *But he* did *die. More than once.*

"He's not Ranger Evans. He's Abraham." Roman licked his lips, his mouth having gone dry. "Abraham." He liked the name — it was old-fashioned and conveyed strength and integrity. It also made Roman warm in a way he couldn't ignore.

Seeing Abraham Evans had been like getting hit with a jolt of electricity. Not a hard hit, not the kind that could kill a person, but the buzzy little *zap* that made one think it sort of tickled.

That fact, combined with a nice, slow-building arousal, kept Roman up all night. He lay in bed, staring up at the stars projected onto his ceiling. They were on the walls too, but he didn't so much as glance to the side. Didn't see the stars after a while, either, as their bright outlines blurred and he had either a vision, or a vivid fantasy.

Abraham was the focus of it. Roman saw him, so strong and silent like before he'd been hurt. There was something inside Abraham, a deep, steady core of strength that shone, a subtle internal glow that seeped out. Almost an aura, but not quite. Roman had never seen anything like it before.

Then Abraham was a spirit, a soul hovering, uncertainty curving his broad shoulders. Roman felt pain so intense he thought he'd pass out. He didn't. Instead he watched as Abraham was pulled back into his body. Roman caught flickers of it happening again, of Abraham wanting to just give up, yet he didn't. Abraham had come back, had lived when he could have chosen to leave this life, to give up on his damaged body and the pain that it held.

What did it take to make such a decision? Roman wished he knew. He believed the spirit was everlasting, that life was a cycle repeated throughout eternity. He'd met old souls, and his calling in life meant that, to him, reincarnation was assured. What one came back as, now *that* wasn't such a clearly defined thing. All Roman knew was, Abraham could have left his life, his battered body that would never be as strong as it once was, and been reborn.

He wondered if, in that moment when Abraham had chosen, he'd seen what his choices were. *Were there options, like man, woman, animal, plant? Air, water, fire, earth? Everything is living, is made of living particles. Do we have a choice in what we're reborn as?*

It was a deep, philosophical question that had always haunted Roman. The idea that one could die and come back as something they'd hate, or some person they'd despise, bothered him.

He put off dwelling on that and let his mind drift back to Abraham himself. Tall, a good foot taller than

Roman's five-three, Abraham *had* been broad-chested and thickly muscled. He'd been a mountain of a man, and Roman had been intimidated by him and, secretly, awed by the former Ranger.

Abraham's short, black hair and tanned skin set off his light, golden brown eyes. The few times Roman had been brave enough to look Abraham in the eyes, he'd noted the unusual color, the amber and almost yellow flecks blended in with the tiniest bits of gray.

Abraham wouldn't have been considered handsome by a lot of people, but he was masculine, without a soft hint to his features, except for those eyes. All sharp angles and rough exterior, that was how Roman thought of him, like chiseled flint made into an arrowhead. Abraham had the wrinkles at the outer edges of his eyes that Roman took to mean he was at least in his thirties. Over a decade older than Roman. The man was, in Roman's opinion, extremely attractive, physically, and maybe in personality, too. Roman didn't know him, not really, though he'd certainly appreciated Abraham's appearance.

Today, however, Abraham had easily looked like he'd aged at warp-speed. Pain had set a black-gray aura hovering around him, and the lines on his face had been more pronounced.

He looked so thin, so much…not smaller, but…but delicate. No, that's not it either. Roman tried closing his eyes, but he saw Abraham in even greater detail then— and he looked like a man hovering on the brink of death. "No."

Sitting up, Roman shook off his exhaustion. A glance at the window to his left, and he knew he'd let his mind wander throughout the night. The soft, orange glow of sunrise was peeking into the room.

Roman got up and turned off the star projector, then he returned to his bed, determined to get a few hours of sleep. He didn't have anything planned for the coming day besides studying and tending his plants, but that didn't mean he needed to be so worn out.

The second he closed his eyes, images of Abraham began flitting through his mind, like a slideshow on the back of his eyelids. Roman didn't fight it. His soul was trying to tell him something, and he'd been ignoring it for too long. Whatever the message, he needed to let it play out, even if it scared him.

The pictures flashed by in timely order, from the first meeting with Ranger Evans, until the last one, with Abraham in the truck. Roman drifted in a sort of sleep state, not quite out of it, yet not awake. He seemed to float throughout space until he was in a dark room, hovering beside a bed.

Roman startled when he raised his head up and found himself entrapped in Abraham's golden gaze.

Abraham's lips moved, forming words that at first had no sound. Then Roman heard him.

"How?" Abraham rasped, his voice thick with the vestiges of sleep. "Dreaming. I must be dreaming." He made a move as if to sit up, and grimaced. Pain swelled out around him. "Fuck. Fuck this being hurt and weak shit, and *fuck* my messed up head, wishing you were really here. You don't want me."

Roman reached out to Abraham with shaking hands, but the transparency of his own form stopped him from actually touching Abraham. Roman was shaken by Abraham's language—he'd never heard the man curse before.

But he didn't really know Abraham, he reminded himself.

Yet there he was, and Roman was suddenly certain that this wasn't a dream or a fantasy, that he'd somehow brought himself, or been brought, into Abraham's home, into his bedroom. This intimate moment meant something, and he couldn't grasp what.

Abraham rubbed his face with his left hand. His right was still, unclenched, in his lap on top of the covers. His aura glowed with pain, and with darker threads of depression and despair.

Roman knew what it was like to lose faith in yourself, to feel betrayed by the body and mind that should have comforted, should have been stronger. He recognized in Abraham the same darkness that still haunted him, though less now than it had in the past. *How much harder is it on a man who has probably thirty-plus years of being strong, being practically unbreakable, to find himself broken after all? It's taken him over a month to be well enough to be discharged from the hospital.*

Abraham tilted his head to one side, and went utterly still.

Roman held his breath, though he didn't know if that was necessary, if what he did there, in Abraham's room, reflected on his body back in his own bed.

Slowly, Abraham turned his head just until those golden eyes were focused on Roman. The sharp inhalation, the way Abraham reached his shaking left hand out to him, amplified those warm, electrical feelings inside Roman.

Roman hadn't felt anything like it in so long, he almost didn't recognize it for what it was — desire, hot and startling, coursing through him. He watched as his hand seemed to float up on its own, under no command of his, until his fingertips brushed over Abraham's.

That electrical current of arousal ramped up to a sharp jolt that sent Roman spiraling away on a gasp.

From one heartbeat to the next, he was snapped into his body, sitting up and panting as he stared sightlessly, trying to get his bearings.

His blood seemed to pump hotter and faster through his veins, and it pooled low in his groin. Roman blinked and blinked until he could focus, until he could *see*, then he looked down at the tented sheet over his hips. Erections were a rarity for him, ever since he'd been assaulted years ago. Sometimes he woke up with one, but this wasn't the same thing at all, nor was it a wet dream, which also happened on occasion. He hadn't come, and his big head wasn't as turned on as his smaller one.

But Roman was surprised, because his dick *was* hard, and unlike all the past experiences where he'd woken up with a hard-on or come in his sleep, he knew exactly why his cock was erect. He knew why he'd grown warm inside and why adrenaline was making his heart pound, his breath short.

He knew why he was drawn to Abraham, and why the man had come to Del Rey — even if Abraham hadn't a clue.

Somehow, some way, Roman had found the one person he never thought would exist. Despite knowing, intellectually, that it wasn't his fault for being assaulted as a thirteen year old, Roman still carried the guilt, the feeling of uncleanliness. It was unreasonable, but not, to his understanding, unusual for victims like him.

So he hadn't thought he'd ever wind up with a mate.

Yet, he had. Abraham Evans had bewitched him since Roman had first laid eyes on him. Roman hadn't ever tried to figure out why. Now he knew.

Abraham Evans was his mate, and somewhere inside the man's bruised and battered soul was something more that called out to Roman and his medicine man side.

Turning away from Abraham wasn't possible. Roman didn't know what he was going to do, how he'd discuss this matter with Abraham, or Miller. And Miller would need to be told—he *was* the pack alpha, after all.

Roman pushed the blankets back and, more out of curiosity than anything else, he wiggled until he had his pajama pants down to mid-thigh. He looked at his cock. It was, he suspected, average in every way, except possibly for not being circumcised. Roman hadn't really paid attention to his penis other than washing it and having to touch it to piss in the past several years. He'd been, necessarily for him, abstinent and completely uninterested in sex. Seeing his dick erect now was interesting, and he ran one fingertip along the head peeking out from the foreskin.

"Oh!" Roman shivered and did it again, eyes nearly rolling because it felt *really* good to touch himself like that. He stopped before he was tempted to go any further. The novelty of being turned on was one he wanted to savor. *Abraham. He turns me on. I want to touch him, kiss him.* Roman kept envisioning Abraham with his beautiful golden eyes, and that pained, wary expression in place. *What would it take to make that go away, to see him, confident, content, once again?*

Roman didn't have the answer. He got out of bed and pulled his pajamas up. He needed to meditate, and think, and let himself heal. Until he was able to move fully from the past, he wouldn't be able to do much for the one man he now knew he had to help.

Heal thyself. I don't know if I can. The truth was, though he knew his part in the pack, Roman had held back, internally, secretly. It was difficult in today's day and age to believe in the Old Ones, the spirits and gods and goddesses his people were born from. Any religion could be and often was mocked, but one that would be viewed as so pagan, especially so.

Though maybe it wasn't religion. Roman had read about plenty of atheists who had been persecuted too.

"It's human nature to fear those different from ourselves, those who think outside the more popular societal parameters." Roman nodded to himself. He knew that was true.

Maybe it was time for him to put his faith in the old ways, and stop resisting his calling. He'd used it for a shelter since he'd stepped into the role of medicine man.

He had to stop playing a role, and become the man he was supposed to be.

Chapter Five

The trips to El Paso were Abraham's least favorite parts of his week. He needed the PT, without a doubt, but he hated going back to the city. Somehow, in the five weeks since he'd moved to Del Rey, the small town had become more of a home to him than anywhere else had ever been. Even the apartment felt like it was his in a way he hadn't experienced before.

He'd considered hiring someone to come to Del Rey twice a week and put him through PT, but that seemed excessive despite his wealth. He prided himself on not throwing money around or letting it be the most important thing in his life. And he'd tried to live off of his earnings as a Texas Ranger. Paying someone to come to Del Rey just went against the kind of man he was, so he tolerated the trips into El Paso.

Plus, he had Gideon, who always seemed eager to take him to El Paso. Gideon said it gave him the opportunity to stock up on art supplies. He never failed to have several bags of purchases when he return to pick Abraham up after PT.

"Looks like you've been doing your exercises," said Monica, his physical therapist. She was about his age, he'd guess, in her mid-thirties, and very no-nonsense. "Make a fist for me."

Abraham gritted his teeth and tried. It was his understanding that he'd suffered irreversible nerve and tissue damage. The best he could hope for was some use of his right hand and arm.

Learning to do everything left-handed was a pain in the ass, but a necessity he had to accomplish.

"Good, good. Again."

He squeezed the ball, his fingers barely moving. "Doesn't look like progress to me."

"It is," Monica stated firmly. "Keep at it. Give me two sets of five reps."

Despite how easy it should have been, physical therapy always left him worn out. He walked out of his appointments disheartened even though he tried not to feel that way.

"Hey, you want to get anything from your apartment here?" Gideon asked. "When's the lease up on it?"

Gideon always asked him if he wanted to go get anything, and Abraham always said no. Abraham thought Gideon was just a tad curious about the place and maybe wanted to snoop just a bit. He'd have been disappointed. There wasn't anything important in that old apartment—but Abraham *had* gotten a voicemail from the apartment manager yesterday and forgotten to call him back.

"Wouldn't hurt to swing by there and get more clothes, I guess," Abraham agreed.

Gideon's shock showed clearly on his face, his eyes widening and his mouth dropping open for a second before he closed it. "Really? I was beginning to think you had some kind of mythical apartment, shrouded in secrecy because…eh. Let's go before you change your mind."

"Ain't anything to see in it, Gid," Abraham assured him. "Not even a picture on the wall anywhere. It's just a place I went to sleep and eat and shower."

"That sounds…awful," Gideon muttered. "Sheesh. Is that part of the lonely Ranger bit? Haha."

"Lone," Abraham corrected, "and no."

Gideon chatted on the drive to the apartments. "You don't mind if I come along, do you?"

"Nah." Abraham unbuckled then got out of the truck. "I think…" He shielded his eyes from the sun. "I think I should have someone pack up my stuff and ship it to Del Rey. I don't think this is my home."

"Yay!" Gideon beamed at him. "You belong with us."

That seemed an odd thing to say, but that was one thing Abraham was slowly becoming aware of — things were different in Del Rey. He couldn't pinpoint it, had no one reason to believe it to be so, yet he felt it inside, that instinct he'd trusted for so long telling him something was up in the small town. It didn't feel bad, or scary, just *off* from everywhere else he'd lived.

Rather than reply to Gideon, Abraham led the way inside to the offices.

"Ranger Evans!" exclaimed the young man working the desk. "Good afternoon! I'll let Janelle know you're here. She just got back from lunch."

Greg? Craig? Gerry? Abraham could never remember his name. "Thanks. I'd appreciate that." He spotted the small plaque on the desk, nearly hidden by a stack of papers. "Malcolm." *Whoa. I was totally off there.*

Malcom leaped up, all enthusiasm and smiles as he blushed. "Anything to help. I'll just go see if she's free. We've had something wrong with our phones today and are hoping they'll be back on soon." He turned and strolled to the manager's office.

Gideon nudged Abraham's left arm. "Someone's got a cru-ush," he sang almost soundlessly.

Abraham glared at him. "Cut it out."

"I'll find your sense of humor yet," Gideon warned him.

That didn't dignify a response. Abraham was tired, not just from the therapy, but from stressing out over everything. He didn't know where he was going in life anymore, and he tended to stay in his apartment and ponder that more often than not. Plus, there were the strange dreams that came to him some nights, or more accurately, some early morning hours. Those dreams felt so real, as if he should be able to reach out and touch Roman. It wasn't possible. What *was* possible was that Abraham was losing his marbles.

"She'll see you now," Malcolm said, snapping Abraham out of his thoughts.

"Thanks." Abraham nodded at Malcolm, then made his way to Janelle's office, with Gideon right behind him.

Janelle stood up to her stately six-foot height, and that was in flats. She was tall and well built, Abraham guessed, though women had never done a thing for him sexually. Even so, there was no mistaking that Janelle was attractive. Her red hair was always styled perfectly, and her makeup done in a way that made her green eyes seem huge.

"Ranger Evans, it's good to see you," Janelle said, offering him her hand.

Abraham felt his cheeks heat as he held out his left hand instead. "Can't use the other one much."

"Oh." Janelle blushed darkly. "Oh, I didn't realize — I'm sorry. I — Oh, I'm just making this all worse. Please, forgive me."

"You didn't know, and for this reason" — he touched his right shoulder with his left hand — "I'm not a Ranger anymore. It's just Abraham."

Janelle frowned. "I'd only heard that you were injured, then nothing more, and the rent is paid through the year, so I didn't know —" She shook her head.

"You couldn't have known the extent of what happened to me," Abraham said, helping her out of the hole they were both tumbling into. "Wasn't anyone around to tell you. I don't think I'll be renewing my lease, however."

"That's too bad," Janelle replied. "You've always been an exemplary renter. We'll miss having you here. I believe your lease is up in two months or so. I was looking yesterday, and I suppose, under the circumstances, if you add your guest to the lease —"

"What guest?" Abraham asked, suspicion making his voice sharp.

Janelle leaned against her desk. "The man who's been staying in your apartment. He told me you sublet it to him, which isn't legal via your contract with us."

Abraham's first impulse was to spin around and run to his apartment. He restrained himself, knowing how dangerous impulsive decisions could be. His mind raced with possibilities, none of which were helpful. "Can you describe him? Did he give you a name?"

Janelle nodded. "Yes, though I'm assuming, from your reaction, you didn't invite anyone to stay in your apartment, much less sublet?"

"Not at all," Abraham agreed, aware of Gideon fidgeting beside him. He could all but smell the nervousness coming from him.

"Okay, well, perhaps we should begin by calling the police first." Janelle reached for her desk phone. "Ah. Let me get my cell."

"I've got one," Gideon offered. "Here." He handed her his phone.

"The man was tall and kind of thin, maybe too thin, and he had several scars on his face and arms," Janelle said as she took the phone then started tapping at the screen.

Abraham and Gideon exchanged worried glances. Anger and something else, something entirely too like fear, threatened to erupt in Abraham. "His name?" he asked again.

"Oh, I wrote it down." Janelle flipped through a pad of paper on her desk. She pushed it toward Abraham just as she began to speak to the person on the phone.

Gentry Vonheimer.

"No. No way."

Abraham wanted to echo Gideon's disbelief, but held his tongue. He'd never heard of Gentry Vonheimer, but he also had no idea how many of the Vonheimer bastards existed.

There'd be fewer of them, if he had his way. Someone was fucking with him, someone evil and dangerous.

Gideon was biting his bottom lip, probably trying to keep from talking about what had happened with the Vonheimers before. Abraham had to live with the betrayal of having one of those fuckers pose and pass as a Texas Ranger. It made him question everyone he'd known through his former job. It should have been impossible for someone to get through the security checks and job requirements it took to be a Ranger, yet a Vonheimer had managed it.

"The police will have someone here as soon as possible," Janelle told them a moment later. "I'm not sure it's much of a priority."

Abraham tipped his chin toward her. "Call them back, and tell them the man in that apartment is responsible for the shooting of a Texas Ranger."

Janelle blanched, her complexion slipping into the ghostly white range. "You?"

"Me," Abraham agreed. "There's every chance he's armed and dangerous—and he might not be alone."

As much as he wanted to go after Vonheimer himself, Abraham had to accept that he wasn't in any shape to do so and come out ahead, or alive. And if Gideon went with him to the apartment, and anything happened to Gideon? It set his teeth on edge, but Abraham stayed put.

With Janelle's second call to the police, sirens soon wailed in the distance.

"Malcolm, we're about to have a situation," Janelle warned. She left the office. Abraham followed her, then bypassed Janelle and Malcolm to stand by the front door.

"This is bad," Gideon whispered. "Why won't those fucking Vonheimers just die already?"

"Nothing good comes easy," Abraham murmured.

The sirens ceased, and Abraham thought someone had some sense by shutting them off before the police vehicles filled the parking lot.

And 'filled the parking lot' was close to an understatement. It looked like every active duty cop in El Paso had come out on the call.

Abraham was aware of Gideon calling Miller, but most of his attention was on the police officers getting out of their vehicles. He opened the door slowly, raising his left hand and keeping it in clear view.

"That's Ranger Evans," said one cop, nodding at him. "I saw him being brought in to the hospital when I was there with my partner." The police officer approached him. "I'm Officer Kyle, and I'm not in charge here, but—the guy who's in the apartment?"

"Very likely responsible for putting me in the hospital, and if it's not him, it's someone working with him," Abraham answered. "He gave the apartment manager a name—said he was Gentry Vonheimer. I've never heard of him, but we couldn't find out much of anything on the Vonheimers before, when I was on the case involving them."

Before Abraham could say anything else, another man began barking out orders and an armored SWAT vehicle pulled up.

"Clear the area." The officer who seemed to be in charge gestured to Abraham. "Get them clear of here now!"

It felt wrong to be on the civilian side of what was happening. Abraham bristled but did as he'd been directed. He wouldn't fuck anything up and cost someone innocent their life.

He and Gideon, along with Malcolm and Janelle, were led by a police officer to what they were told was a safe place. There, Abraham and Janelle were grilled repeatedly about what had happened.

Which was how Abraham found out that other residents of the apartments had claimed to have seen a man coming and going from Abraham's place for weeks.

It sent a shiver down his spine, but more than that, it infuriated him to know that his home had been so easily invaded—even if the apartment there wasn't his home anymore.

And he wondered how long he'd been played for a fool, and what the Vonheimers' endgame was. *And how many of them there are, because goddamn, they should all be dead. Except two or more got away. No one could say for sure how many scents the tracking dogs picked up.*

That was one of the things that kept him up at night, and not because he feared for himself—but because as long as the men who'd hurt Roman years ago were on the loose, as long as there was even a *chance* that any of them were still alive, Abraham couldn't relax completely. Roman might still be spooked around him, and Abraham hardly saw a glimpse of him on occasion when heading to one of his PT appointments. It didn't matter. He had come to accept that he'd lay down his own life for the young man without hesitation.

Chapter Six

Miller came running out of his office in the gallery. Every fine hair on Roman's nape stood up in the age-old sign of alarm.

"Miller? What's going on?" he asked, rushing over to follow Miller outside.

"Tell the Fervent Five to stay inside and watch the place," Miller ordered, his back to Roman as he ran for his truck. "You stay, too."

"No." Roman didn't know what was going on, but it had to do with him, somehow. Him, or Abraham, who he'd visited every morning in that trance-like state he'd discovered.

"I've gotta get to El Paso," Miller snapped. "I ain't got time for arguing."

"Stay and watch the gallery," Roman turned and shouted to Kyra and Paul, who had followed them outside. "We'll be back."

"You're not going with me!" Miller jerked open the driver's side door.

Roman opened the passenger one. "What's going on?"

"Don't you get in—"

Roman climbed up onto the seat.

"God damn it, Ro," Miller growled. "Get. Out!"

"No," Roman said again, though he wanted to obey Miller on some level. It was a shifter's instinct, he decided, and while he couldn't shift, he *was* still a coyote shifter and member of a pack, of which Miller was the alpha. But he was also the pack medicine man. "No. I won't."

"Roman," Miller began.

"You're wasting time arguing," Roman pointed out, buckling his seatbelt. "Whatever's going on, I need to be there. Are you going to tell me I'm not supposed to be going, when everything inside of me says otherwise?"

Miller started the truck and slammed his door so hard the vehicle rocked. "You telling me you need to go?"

"I'm telling you, you aren't going without me. How often do I give you trouble now, Miller?" Roman pointed out. "I don't argue. I study, I meditate, I pray and practice making tinctures and herbal mixtures for everything I can think of."

"You got one to keep any living Vonheimers away?" Miller demanded in a slightly mean tone. "'Cause that's what we're going to El Paso for. Seems someone claiming to be a Gentry Vonheimer's been using Abraham's apartment."

Roman's entire body went cold with fear, and memories he didn't want tried to rip into his head. *No. No! Enough! I've lost too many years to them already.*

"Get out," Miller said again. "You don't need to go."

"I do," Roman said through gritted teeth. "Where's Abraham?"

"Why're you asking?" Miller retorted. "You won't even wave to the man when we drive past, and he looks at you like—"

"He's in El Paso, at his apartment," Roman muttered, feeling even colder. His hands ached from him clenching them.

"He's not in his apartment," Miller said. "Him and Gid are with some police officers while SWAT takes Abraham's apartment to pieces. Abraham and Gid are safe. They're safe."

Then Roman would be, too. "I'm not getting out, and you're wasting time."

Miller cursed and whipped the steering wheel to the left. The truck's tires squealed as the vehicle shot out and onto the street.

Roman didn't say a word. He thought instead about the way he'd become comfortable with his odd visits, how he spent a few minutes some mornings watching Abraham.

For the most part, he didn't think Abraham was aware of what was happening, or if he was, he might have believed the visits to have been dreams. Sometimes Abraham's eyes opened just a bit, and once, Abraham had moved as if to touch him, though Abraham hadn't been looking at him as far as Roman had been able to discern.

But Roman wasn't sure he was asleep. In fact, he didn't know what was happening during those times, except that he had to be near Abraham, and that was the only manner in which he could deal with it.

Roman glanced at Miller through his lashes, trying not to be obvious. *Should I ask him about it? He's my alpha, and he's not a jerk. He's been there for me, always.*

"Miller?"

Miller grunted.

Roman took a deep breath then let it out. "I think he's my mate. Abraham, I mean."

Miller jerked, and the truck swerved before Miller corrected his steering. "What? Say that again."

Roman gulped and wiped at his suddenly sweaty brow. "I-I think he's my m-mate. I get a-aroused—" He couldn't say any more along those lines, and his face felt like it was on fire. He ducked his head.

"When you think about him?" Miller asked, his voice squeaking at the end.

"Yeah." Roman scrubbed at his hot cheeks. "I dream about him, and I…I think I do some sort of dream state-astral projection thing, into his bedroom."

"Jesus," Miller muttered.

"I've done it a few times," Roman added. "It's like I have to be close to him, and that's the way I can handle it."

"Jesus Christ," Miller said. "That's… Roman, that's creepy, like Peeping Tom creepy."

"No! It's not like that!" *Is it? Oh gods, am I a creeper?*

Miller glanced sideways at him. "Are you sure you're actually, you know, um. There?"

Roman bit his bottom lip and nodded. When he let his lip slide free, he said, "I've been reading up on it, actually. You remember the book you and Gideon gave me about a month ago? The old one?" The one he had to read while wearing special gloves and that he was transcribing onto his laptop, sketching the drawings out and uploading them… "It has information in there you wouldn't believe." Which reminded him of something. "It also mentions an older text, one I want to try to hunt down a copy of, if possible. But anyway." He flapped a hand, chasing off the misdirection. "Yes, a medicine man—or woman—should be able to use dream visitation and astral projection to send their spirit off for short trips. Well, later, with more experience, distance and time aren't supposed to be issues, but I can't even grasp that yet."

"Time travel?" Miller shook his head. "Really?"

Roman shrugged. "It's not my place to doubt it when what's in me has shown that it's true. Maybe not the time travel or great distances, but if I can slip out of myself to be around the one man I actually want, then why wouldn't anything else be possible?"

"Why not, indeed." Miller huffed, and his cheeks puffed up then hollowed as he exhaled. "Fuck, that's just weird, Ro. I mean, okay. I get that we lost our ability to shift and such because we strayed so far from our original spiritualness—spirituality—but…I don't know how much I can believe."

"Maybe that's okay, as long as *I* believe." Roman wouldn't go into detail about the other, less likely to be believed things he had glimpsed in the book, *Argu Challan*. He didn't know what the title meant, either. There was no description. It was just a lot of information and spells, advice and guidance for a shaman or medicine person to learn. And it was written in a weird dialect of English that Roman couldn't figure out the roots of.

"I'd like to try and track down the companion book it mentions," Roman said.

"Go for it. Have Gid help you. He gets off on research." Miller's mouth tipped up on one side. "Literally, sometimes."

"Ack!" Roman laughed. "I don't need to know that."

"And I probably shouldn't have said it." Miller glanced at him again. "So, tell me about this deal with Abraham. And, um, I guess why you mentioned being, you know, turned on. By it. Him." Miller groaned. "Man, I'm a total failure at the father-figure stuff."

"It's an awkward subject to talk about," Roman began. "Sex, I mean. For me, at least. I haven't had any interest in it as an adult. Abraham... He's always made me uncomfortable."

"And *that* makes you think he's your mate?" Miller asked.

Roman struggled for the words to explain. "I didn't understand why he made me feel that way. Hot and scared, cold and fluttery inside. It confused me. *He* confused me."

"He's a good ten or fifteen years older than you, at least," Miller pointed out.

"So? That doesn't bother me, and maybe—" Roman rubbed at his stomach as he grew more nervous. "Maybe that's what I need. Someone not in the same age range as me."

Miller didn't say anything for a few minutes, then, "Okay. I can see that, actually, plus, Abraham's got this whole code of honor thing going on. I don't think he moved to Del Rey for shits and giggles. Now that you told me this, especially."

"You think he's here because of me," Roman said.

"To protect you, except he ain't quite up to much yet." Miller took his cell phone from his pocket and handed it to Roman. "Text Gid for me, let him know we're gonna be there soon."

At the speed Miller was driving, they'd be there in seconds. Roman snorted and sent the text to Gideon, adding, *Is Abraham okay? This is Roman asking.*

"Okay, sent." Roman started to set the phone down but it vibrated. "He texted back."

"Read it."

"He just said that they're fine, away from any danger, and the SWAT team already did their thing, as far as he can tell." Roman handed the phone over.

"Just hold it for me," Miller said. "I shouldn't touch that thing when I'm doing ninety."

The speed limit was seventy-five or eighty along the stretch of I-10 they were on. Roman could never remember which, and it wouldn't have mattered either way. If they wrecked at seventy-five, eighty or ninety, they were dead.

"Be careful," he urged. "So, is it okay with you that Abraham's my mate?"

"Are you positive he is?" Miller asked.

Roman nodded. "Yes, I mean, I think I am. I've never had a mate, obviously, but I did a reading on it, and I used the pendulum and read my tea leaves. All signs point to a great big yes."

"And the traveling to his bedroom, how do you think he'll feel about that?"

"I don't know," Roman admitted. "Probably as weirded out as he'll feel when I tell him we're shifters. Then can't prove it because I can't shift."

Miller laughed. "Aw, now, Ro, you'll get there, and you can borrow me and Gid for a demo when you feel that Abraham can be trusted with that secret."

"Thanks. There's something else," Roman added, looking out of the window. "I don't think he's fully human."

"What?" Miller must have leaned over, because he poked Roman in the arm. "What was that?"

Roman yelped and swatted at him. "Don't do that when you're driving like you're on a race track!"

"Calm down. We weren't gonna wreck, and I didn't look away from the road. I just leaned a little and jabbed at you. I won't let us get hurt, Ro."

"Okay." Roman took a couple of breaths. "Sorry."

"Nah, it's fine. So tell me why you don't think he's human," Miller said. "Fully."

Something about the way Miller spoke, his pose so casual, like he wasn't surprised. But he'd sounded startled at first, and Roman wondered if that was because Miller hadn't known, or he'd been surprised that Roman had figured it out. Roman was leaning toward the latter. He knew that Miller was very smart. "You know."

Miller tapped the steering wheel with his fingertips. "Suspected. Not at first, but later, yeah. Couldn't put my finger on what it was about Abraham that made him seem so...so *different*, I guess, than the other humans we're around. Thought it was his gruff Ranger act, you know. And he smells a little like something wild. Can't tell you what, or if he's for sure a shifter, but I suspect he is, and like us, he doesn't have the ability to shift. Could be he's even unaware of it if he *is* a shifter. I don't know. What's your read on it?"

Roman hadn't been close enough to Abraham to really scent him, and even so, the acute senses shifters had, or should have, weren't all up to par on Roman yet. He had grown stronger, and it frustrated him to no end that he, as the pack medicine man, wasn't in touch with his coyote spirit like he should have been. It was a source of anger and worry for him.

So all he had to go on were his instincts, and they'd been pinging for Abraham for a while before Roman's brain had caught on. "Well, I can't say just why. You know I can't shift. I don't have all the heightened senses yet, though they've gotten better. I haven't been around Abraham in person, not really, so I don't know what he smells like. It's just a feeling, like there's something inside of him, calling out to me, as a medicine man, not just as a mate. I wonder if I'm reading him wrong. Maybe you should ask him about his parents."

Miller barked out a laugh. "Aw, hell no. I met those folks. They were the snootiest assholes I've had to tolerate in a long time. Abraham ain't too fond of them, I don't think. They sure were standoffish, and from what I understand, mad as hell he wouldn't move in with them or something like that. I think there's money involved—he's got it, they want it."

"You think he's rich?" Roman asked, unable to connect vast amounts of wealth to the weathered, rough former Ranger who looked more like a blue-collar worker than someone who'd wear a suit and tie.

"Does that make a difference to you?"

Does it? Miller could be wrong, anyway. "It's kind of a moot point. I don't know if I can be his mate, but there's this...this *wanting* in me, this hunger for him that seems to be overriding all the fear that lingered."

Miller signaled for an upcoming exit. "You stopped going to therapy, and you won't take the online sessions. Maybe you ought to reconsider. There's even sex therapists, man, I don't know what they're officially called, but... Jesus. Maybe you shouldn't listen to me about that."

Roman couldn't stop himself from smiling. Miller was so uncomfortable talking to him about anything having to do with sex, but he was trying, and that made Roman feel good—loved and valued. "Actually, I found someone to talk to. Another shifter, a wolf shaman, actually, if you can believe that. He came to me in a dream, and at first I thought it was just that—a dream. Then I tried the phone number that kept bouncing around in my head. It's been a strange month to say the least, Miller."

"And you didn't see fit to tell me about this shaman guy sooner?" Miller demanded. "He could be some loony rip-off artist. Well, except for the whole dream thing. And the phone number being right. Actually, that'd scare the shit out of me. I don't think I'd ever make it as a medicine man or whatever."

"I didn't mention it, no, because it's personal, and he's helped me, a lot. He's very powerful, like you wouldn't believe." Roman glanced down as the phone vibrated again. "I think I can learn a lot from him, and he's actually in South Texas when he isn't off somewhere else."

"Is that another text from Gid?"

Roman read the message. "Yeah, he says they're still fine, and Abraham's apartment was empty but trashed. They'll probably have to go to the police station and if they leave before we'll get there, Gideon will let us know where to go. And he said that Abraham didn't seem so agitated after he got my message. I just asked if Abraham was okay." Roman's pulse raced.

"That probably means a lot coming from you, when you've hidden from Abraham for months now," Miller pointed out. "Plus, he must know you're coming with me, and if he's been aware of those visits you told me about, well, maybe he's found himself some hope where there wasn't much before."

Roman didn't know if he was the source of Abraham's hope, if that was what Abraham felt, but he wanted to be. He wanted to be that good, shiny beacon for such a strong, steady man.

It fed Roman's soul, to think about being the best part of someone's life. *Not someone. Abraham Evans. I want to be the brightest spot, the warmth in his soul, and I want to feel that for him.*

Which meant that Roman was making progress, and working through the past once again. He wouldn't give up on himself this time. Not when the cost would be one that not only Roman, but Abraham would have to pay.

"I never thought about having a mate," Roman said after a few minutes of silence. "I would have sworn I never wanted one, but now… I think I do."

"You think so, huh?" Miller chuckled. "Well, you don't rush anything. The hormones flaring up between mates can make ya fuck first and talk way, *way* later. You and Abraham ought to take it slow, if you can. Though, I'm guessing this has been building between ya'll for months now. Maybe since the first time he interviewed you?"

Roman remembered the chills he'd felt, the confusing emotions that he now was coming to understand were desire for Abraham. "Yeah, I think so."

"I'm here if you need to talk about anything, Ro," Miller said. "I mean, *anything.* In fact, maybe it's time we make plans to get together and have that birds and bees talk all kids should have with their parents, or in this case, your alpha. Unless you want to talk to your mom."

"No, no I don't. She'd tell my sister, and I'd never hear the end of it." Roman's older sister had chilled out some in the past couple of years, but she still wasn't someone he'd trust, and she wasn't his friend.

"Well then, I reckon I can brave my way through it, though talking about sex with you might embarrass us both. Don't know if Gid would be a good add to that conversation or not, but I'd lean toward yes, even though he's really, er, *enthusiastic* about sharing details I wish he wouldn't." Miller sighed. "Oh well. I can stand to be mortified for you, kiddo. You're like my own son, you know."

Happiness washed over Roman. "Thanks. That means a lot." Especially since his own dad was long gone, having left back when Roman was just a baby. Roman had never heard a word from the jerk.

But at least he had Miller, and Gideon, and a pack that really did care about him.

And Abraham. I might just be able to have him, too. It was a goal worth working toward.

Chapter Seven

Walking out of the police station would have gone a lot smoother had Abraham not felt a prickle of awareness that drew his gaze to the left. The moment his eyes locked on Roman, Abraham's feet seemed to have gotten confused over their purpose. He stumbled and, unable to reach out with his right hand, would have fallen had Gideon not flung an arm around his waist.

"Easy, now, Abe, no need to trip on air," Gideon teased.

Abraham hated the nickname 'Abe', but would have hated to hurt Gideon's feelings even more, so he didn't remark upon it. "Seems like what happened. Tripped over nothing."

Gideon grinned. "Or you tripped over your tongue. What's with you and Roman? I swear you two just electrified the room."

Abraham didn't want to discuss something he himself didn't understand. "Dunno. I'm tired, though, and Janelle isn't going to give me back my deposit after the mess left in the apartment. Guess I don't blame her."

"Hmph! You can't tell me that property isn't insured," Gideon said.

"Doesn't matter." Abraham's voice abandoned him as they came to a stop by Roman and Miller.

"Hey, hon, Abraham." Miller nodded to him after smiling at Gideon. "Roman came along, obviously."

"Hi, Abraham," Roman whispered.

Abraham couldn't have said what, if anything, had changed between them. He wanted to ask Roman about those morning visits, but he was afraid he'd sound crazy, and he didn't want to scare Roman off when he'd finally come close.

So he settled for an equally quiet, "Hello, Roman. How are you?"

Roman's eyes glittered and Abraham was struck once again by Roman's fragile beauty, though he knew Roman had more strength than most people.

"What happened?" Miller interjected just as Roman's lips parted. "Tell me from the beginning, Abraham."

"Can we get to the truck first? I'm beat," Abraham admitted, then regretted doing so in front of Roman. Then again, he had no right to be posturing. It would be dishonest to act like something he wasn't—whole, unbroken, not hurting, when he wasn't any of those things. "I need a couple of pain pills, and they're in the glovebox."

Miller bobbed his head. "Yeah, I reckon I can wait a few minutes to get the details. Though I'm taking it that Vonheimer wasn't caught?"

"No, and I don't recognize this particular Vonheimer. Janelle, the apartment manager, described him and someone here sketched him out. Didn't look like anyone I'd seen before, though there was a resemblance, I guess. Gideon said there was." Abraham would let Gideon explain that part.

Which he did promptly. "It's the eyes, those beady, weaselly eyes. And the jaw."

Roman didn't say a word, but seemed to shrink into himself somehow. Then Miller put an arm around Roman's shoulders. "It's okay, Ro. It's all gonna be okay. No reason to think this guy'd be after you, and it was Abraham's apartment he was at. Seems like maybe this particular Vonheimer is trying to piss you off, Abraham."

"He did that, sure enough," Abraham conceded, keeping a close watch on Roman. Strangely enough, there was a tiny freckle on Roman's top lip that Abraham had noticed the first morning he'd dreamed of Roman being in his room. He must have noticed it, at least subconsciously, at some point before being hurt.

"We've got to get both trucks back to Del Rey, so why don't we go grab a bite after you take your meds, then we can talk over dinner?" Miller suggested. "That okay with you, Roman?"

"It's fine." Roman smiled just a bit and Abraham's heart nearly pounded right out of his chest. Then Roman turned his head, and that slip of a smile was aimed at Abraham.

Abraham forgot to breathe as he stared. Someone grabbed him by the left arm and began tugging. Abraham shook his head and knew his own smile was a wry one. Gideon had a hold of him and was smirking, too. *Smug bastard.*

"Ro can ride with me," Miller said once they were outside. "Get your pain meds, Abraham, and we'll talk when we get to Jalascio's."

"I-I can drive," Roman offered, glancing quickly at Abraham. "I have my license."

"You haven't driven in El Paso before, have you?" Miller asked. "And it's rush hour. Best you save the driving for later."

Roman pursed his lips but didn't argue.

Abraham got his pain pills swallowed and washed down with a bottle of water that'd become nauseatingly hot while sitting in the truck for hours.

"Sorry y'all had to wait," Gideon was saying. "The cops took *forever* asking questions. Like we had answers to why that fuckwad was in Abraham's apartment! Sheesh!"

Roman glanced his way, and Abraham felt something warm and welcome spread out from his core. For a moment, he halfway expected to be transformed by it, though that was a silly thought he put down to being in pain and confused on top of that. *Why did Roman come here, with Miller? Why now, when he's always shied away from me? Except that day in the truck, but even then he was skittish.*

It was a puzzle he couldn't figure out, and he let himself be nudged into the truck so they could get away from the police station.

But Abraham didn't look away from Roman, watching him through barely open eyes. He didn't want to be obvious about it, yet he was unable to stop himself. To see Roman so close, to have heard him speak, and there'd been that little hint of a smile... Abraham was more besotted than ever, and he figured he was just going to be hung up on Roman, be the bearer of unrequited love, probably for the rest of his life.

Denying that he loved Roman was futile. Believing that Roman would ever want him, love him in return was more than he could hope for at this point.

"So, explain about Roman," Gideon said as soon as he got behind the steering wheel. "Don't *even* think you can blow me off this time. The only other instances of that kind of *kaboom* electrical attraction I've ever been around was when I found my own mate…er, man." Gideon coughed. "Talk, Oh Stoic One."

Abraham surprised himself with a laugh. "Oh Stoic One?"

"Well, you just ruined it by laughing," Gideon griped, though he didn't really sound upset about it. He started the truck, then pulled out of the parking spot. "But I guess you can have a pass on that. Spill."

Strangely enough, Abraham found himself doing just that. "I don't know what to say except, I got the case, Roman's case, and I read that file and wanted to kill the men that hurt him. I've always been a believer in justice, in the law, but this was different. This was so much anger I really did want to commit murder, and that wasn't like me. Scared me, to tell the truth, though I wrangled that unreasonable reaction down. Then I met Roman, and he— I—" *How to explain?*

"You met him, and it was like finding the missing piece of your heart?" Gideon asked as he drove down a busy street.

Abraham almost laughed again, except Gideon sounded sincere, not joking at all. "I don't know about that, but there was something intangible, something that wouldn't let me put him squarely in the victim category, strictly in a case to be solved and filed away. I dreamed of him after the first time I met him. He was laughing, and lit up with joy, not somber and scared like he is around me. I've dreamed that same one over and over, and I can't shake feeling like I have to take care of him, keep him safe. Like if he's not ever happy, that's my failing."

"Ah. That... Hmm." Gideon cleared his throat. "That sounds like what I went through on some level when I met Miller. The emotion, I mean. We were all over each other pretty quick, though I can see why with Roman...that...wouldn't...er, work."

"We can talk around it, but that don't make it go away," Abraham said, his stomach twisting with nausea. "He was raped, beaten, hurt badly. It's been years but the scars something like that leaves behind don't ever go away."

Gideon tutted. "Hey, it sounds like you're consigning Roman to the part of permanent victim, and there's a hell of a lot more to the man than victim, anyway. I know he went through something more horrible than most people can imagine, but people *do* heal and have normal lives after things like that happen. After being raped," Gideon added. "It's hard to say that word, you know? Especially in relation to someone I love, and Roman is like my little brother. That's not the point, though. The point is, or part of my point, rather, is that you seem stuck on him being the victim, on what happened in his past, and I'm not downplaying that, but you should maybe consider that he is really strong, and he can overcome his past. He's been working on that for years now. Maybe have some faith in him, is all."

Abraham didn't have a retort, because he saw the truth in what Gideon was telling him. They remained in companionable silence until they arrived at the restaurant. Then Gideon made small talk while they got out of the truck and met up with Miller and Roman, and again while they waited to be seated.

Roman took the seat beside him, and Abraham couldn't quite stifle a small gasp of surprise. He could feel the warmth of Roman's body heat, saw the slight trembling of his fingers as Roman took the menu from the waitress.

Abraham nearly dropped his own menu, feeling clumsy himself. At least he managed to open it while asking the waitress for water and a cup of coffee. He was getting the fuzzy-headed feeling that came on after taking his pain meds. The pain itself became endurable but his brain felt like slush.

"All right, tell me," Miller said.

Abraham looked at Gideon.

"Uh, you do it. It's your apartment, after all." Gideon pointed at him.

"Former," Abraham corrected. "That lease is terminated." Focusing on what information he had, he continued. "Janelle had left me a voice message yesterday saying she needed to speak with me. Figured since were in El Paso today, it'd be okay to swing by there, pack a few more clothes, and let Janelle know I don't plan on moving back there." He heard Roman's soft inhale, as if he were surprised but trying to hide it. "I'd like to stay in Del Rey for a while, at least. I don't know yet what I'm going to do once PT is over and done with, but that's not important right now."

Miller smiled crookedly. "You're welcome to stay in Del Rey and make it your home for good. You're my friend, and Gid's, too. We consider you one of our own."

That bit of friendliness and acceptance soothed a part of Abraham that he'd not known was hurting. "Thanks. That means a lot." He felt like he should have more to say, but what that would be, exactly, escaped him. "I'll have to figure out something to do. Can't be idle, or I'll go crazy." Then he forced himself to focus on what they'd been discussing before then. "When Janelle told me that someone claimed I'd sublet the apartment to them, then she gave me his name, Gentry Vonheimer, I wanted to go rushing up there and kick in the door. I've accepted that I'm not...up to doing any such thing. Figured it was my pride or Vonheimer getting away. Which he did regardless. SWAT and several cops arrived, but when they broke into the apartment, it was empty. The place had been trashed."

"How'd no one hear that when it was happening?" Miller asked.

Abraham had to give him credit for being quick on the draw. "Good question. The damage was done in a controlled manner, as far as the investigating officers could tell. Walls shredded up with box cutters, same for the carpet. Most of the appliances had been damaged, the paint corroded off of them. Just things that wouldn't have made noise." He glanced at Roman, needing to make sure Roman wasn't about to bolt.

But Roman didn't look scared. He appeared to be angry, his pale skin flushed and his eyes narrowed, his full lips thinned in a frown. He was stunning, and for a moment, all Abraham could do was stare.

It was strange, but he could have sworn he smelled an acrid aroma that reminded him of anger. *Must be something burning in the kitchen, fajitas or maybe carnitas.*

Either Miller or Gideon cleared their throat, and Abraham jolted like he'd been poked in the ribs. His own cheeks were hot with a blush, as embarrassed as he was for being caught gawking at Roman.

"Food's here," Miller said, gesturing to the waitress. "So Vonheimer got away."

"And I didn't recognize the bastard. Neither did Gideon," Abraham confirmed, glad to not be getting lectured. He knew he was too old and too...too *everything* for Roman. That didn't seem to stop Abraham from wanting him, from needing to protect him.

From slipping into love with him more and more each day.

Abraham was a mess, emotionally and physically, but what he felt for Roman had never wavered or decreased since the moment he'd first met the man.

"What I don't get is, what do these Vonheimer assholes have out for us and our pack—er, our...uh...uh—" Gideon picked up his burrito and shoved it in his mouth.

Pack. The word resonated in Abraham, though he didn't know why. And Gideon's reaction, just like Miller's—who'd gone stiff for a second, shooting Gideon a warning glare before digging into his own food—had both seemed a little strange. Something about that word had them both nervous.

Abraham checked Roman in his peripheral vision and shivered, slowly turning his head to face Roman, who shifted in his chair, until he was staring directly at Abraham.

There was more green than usual in Roman's eyes, chasing out almost all of the brown. Abraham could have sat there studying every facet, every shade of green and striation in Roman's irises, except he had enough sense to realize that'd be creepy.

Then Roman's eyes crinkled slightly at the outer edges, and Abraham's heart just about stopped on him as he lowered his gaze enough to see all of Roman's face, and the shy smile just gracing his lips.

In that moment, nothing and no one else existed in Abraham's world. It was a memory made and embedded in his mind—the way the lighting accentuated Roman's cheek bones and the tip of his nose, the thick, dark fringe of lashes around his eyes. There was the freckle on Roman's lip, and a few barely discernible ones across the bridge of his nose. This close, Abraham could see that Roman's lips were slightly chapped, but pink like fresh raspberries. His skin looked smooth, as if he never had to shave, and Abraham wanted to kiss him, a gentle brush of his mouth over Roman's.

But despite how entranced he was, he still knew better than to do such a thing in a crowded dive like Jalascio's.

Roman averted his gaze and Abraham forced himself to stop staring. He had never in his life felt anything as powerful as whatever had just passed between him and Roman.

Strange things were happening all around him, and he needed to be alone, needed time to think.

And he needed to know why he was beginning to think he hadn't been dreaming of Roman on the mornings when he'd appeared to be in Abraham's bedroom, how he'd known there was a miniscule freckle on Roman's top lip. He didn't think it was because of a subconscious memory anymore.

Something was going on, and Miller, Gideon and Roman knew what it was, were a part of it. Abraham intended to find out just what secret they were keeping.

Chapter Eight

The following day, Roman found himself pacing the length of the nursery, trying to work up the courage to go talk to Abraham, alone. It wasn't that he thought he wouldn't be safe with Abraham—on the contrary, he didn't believe for one second that Abraham would ever hurt him.

It was more that he was scared of making a fool out of himself, of wanting something, and reaching for it, only to fall flat on his face.

"But if he's really my mate—no, he *is* my mate, then he won't reject me. In theory." Roman groaned and stopped walking. "Gods, why does this have to be so *hard*?" And it wasn't just taking action that was proving to be hard, his penis had been in that state more often than not since the moment he'd sat beside Abraham at the restaurant yesterday.

In fact, Roman had been so twisted up about being aroused and trying to figure out how to deal with this new scenario, that he hadn't been able to concentrate or drift off into that astral plane or dream state. He hadn't slipped away to check on Abraham, and he was worried about him.

It was impossible not to be when Abraham was still so clearly suffering. He'd put on a little weight, but was much thinner than he'd been before being hurt, and it broke Roman's heart to think of Abraham alone in his apartment all the time.

Miller had told Roman that Abraham rarely went anywhere other than to PT. Gael and Iker visited him, as did other pack members, but that wasn't the same as getting *out*. Roman did know something about holing up when one was injured. He'd wanted to stay hidden in his bedroom forever after he'd been assaulted. Between his mom and Miller, though, Roman had moved past the need to hide all the time.

Or did I? I spend days on end here in the ceremonial hall. People come to visit, or check up on me. The Fervent Five hang around, but they're usually not right here with me. Am I still hiding?

The idea that he hadn't progressed as far as he'd believed irked Roman. He strode from the nursery to his little office, and sat long enough to fire off a question to the shaman who had befriended him, asking for his thoughts about the whole hiding thing.

Then he couldn't be bothered to wait for an answer. Impulsiveness wasn't something Roman gave way to often, but the need to see Abraham was growing stronger with each minute. He understood that it was because they were mates, and spending time with Abraham yesterday, sitting so close to him, smelling him, hearing him, seeing him — all those had combined to pull taut the lines of attraction the mate bond had created. *Will create. We haven't mated, haven't had sex.*

When Roman thought of Abraham touching him, he felt warm and *good* and he liked that, very much. He didn't know how he'd handle being touched in a sexual way, and he wouldn't as long as he kept himself out of Abraham's reach.

That was something he didn't want to do anymore.

Excited, scared—and with anticipation bubbling up over both of those emotions—Roman trotted to his bedroom and started digging through his dresser drawers. He wanted to look good, attractive for his mate.

He found a faded pair of jeans that weren't too tight or too loose. He'd ditched his skinny jeans a while back, tired of having them cut off the circulation to his legs or other parts. Roman much preferred not having to have any part of his body amputated due to lack of blood flow.

He picked out a soft gray T-shirt, then spent five minutes trying to find a matching pair of socks that didn't have either stains or holes in them. He hated socks and preferred to go barefoot or wear flip-flops. Neither of those seemed like sexy options.

Roman laid out his clothes on the bed, then set his Paint Splatter Doc Martens by them. He'd only worn the boots once, and they didn't have so much as a speck of dust on them. A matte black leather belt completed the outfit. Roman nodded to himself, pleased with his selections, but something was off.

"Oh!" He laughed at himself. "Underwear. Duh."

Fortunately, he had better underwear than socks. He tossed a silky-feeling pair of gray briefs onto the bed.

Then he went into the bathroom, and gave himself a looking over in the mirror. His blond hair was a mess, which meant he'd probably forgotten to brush it after he'd woken up. There were slight bags under his eyes from the sleepless night. Even so, he didn't look too rough. Shaving wasn't necessary—he'd never had so much as peach fuzz on his face.

Roman brushed his teeth—because he couldn't remember if he'd bothered with that, either—and followed that up with a quick but thorough shower. Once he was convinced he was clean, he finished up in the bathroom, ignoring his half-hard dick, and went to get dressed.

He'd been tempted to masturbate in the shower, but hadn't given in. He wanted to present himself as he was to Abraham. There was, he knew, a chance that Abraham would look at him and see the broken boy he'd been years ago, not the man he'd become.

Roman wasn't going to let that happen.

After he dressed and had his Docs on, Roman returned to the bathroom and brushed his hair, then blow dried it. He had it smooth and soft after a few minutes, and he decided his hair looked as good as possible.

One more check in the mirror, and he gave himself a thumbs up. "You can do this." He left the bathroom and took a moment in his bedroom to try to calm his rapidly beating heart.

Meditation helped. He knew that. Roman lowered himself to the floor, sitting in his favored position for meditating, and let himself sink into that restful state. It was easier than he'd thought it'd be with all the worry and need tangling up in him.

It was easier, because he knew he was doing the right thing. He needed Abraham, and Abraham needed him. If he trusted in his instincts, in the old ways and the path he was taking, Roman needed to do so fully.

He let go of the pieces of worry and fear, sending them away from him with every exhalation, small puffs of dirty brown-gray clouds he envisioned clearing out from his mind and heart, from his soul. It was a method he used when he wanted to get something that was bothering him out of the way, some emotion or fear. It didn't always do the job completely, but it helped.

When he'd found his center and his peace, Roman brought himself out from his meditative state, then took another minute to ease up off the floor. He felt much calmer, surer of his path. Roman let the peace of his decision comfort him as he left his bedroom. He stopped by his office and saw that the shaman had replied.

"Trust your instincts instead of fighting them, and let your soul soar. You are stronger than your fears, stronger than your past," he read out loud, touched by that part of the reply.

Roman was strengthened even more by the shaman's faith in him.

"I'll be back later," Roman said to Kyra and Frisky, who were on the porch outside. Paul, Tandy and Brandt were sprawled out on a blanket under a tree fifty feet or so away.

"Where are you going?" Kyra asked, frowning. "You never go anywhere dressed up like that."

How bad was it that jeans and a nice T-shirt, and killer Docs, meant he was dressed up? Roman snorted. "Well, I'm going to see Abraham."

Kyra sprung out of her chair like she'd been ejected, all bouncing energy. "Oh cool! Let me just get the others—"

Roman held up one hand to stop her. "No. This is personal. I'm sorry but y'all need to let me do this alone."

Kyra went back to frowning. "Now, Roman. You know we're supposed to stay with you, as Miller asked us to do."

"And I appreciate that, but no one is going with me to Abraham's. What I need to say to him is personal," he reiterated.

"We can follow you in and wait at the gallery," she said after a moment. "As long as Miller says that's okay."

"He will." Roman didn't argue with her. He was able to make a concession, as long as he got to go to Abraham. "I'm going to start my car and get the AC going." He didn't want to be a sweat-ball by the time he arrived at Abraham's, and while the day had yet to get hot, it'd happen soon enough.

Roman trotted down the steps and walked around to the side of the building, where his small car was parked beside Kyra's SUV. His car was old and the paint was peeling, but the AC worked and the engine ran, so he was content with it.

He unlocked the car and got in, started the engine and the AC. There'd been a time when locking his car hadn't been something he'd done, but with the Vonheimers having caused trouble in the past, he'd started locking it.

He backed the car up until he could turn it around. Kyra and the rest of the crew headed to the SUV. Roman waved at them. He hadn't doubted that Miller would be okay with him going to talk to Abraham.

Roman just needed to figure out what to say. He wasn't going to worry about it, though. *Trust your instincts.* That was exactly what he was going to do. No more fighting them, no more fear.

Chapter Nine

The knock on his door didn't surprise Abraham. It seemed as if someone came to check on him every few hours on the days when he was feeling his worst. After a restless night, and his trying to wean himself off his pain meds somewhat, Abraham would have said feeling like warm shit was several steps above how he felt.

But when he opened his door without bothering to check the peephole, and found Roman standing there, Abraham was so surprised that he felt dizzy at first. He stood gripping the doorknob with his left hand, his right useless except for a twitch. The urge to touch Roman was strong, but not one he could give into. Instead he just stared, mouth open until he realized he was slack-jawed. Abraham closed his mouth with an audible snap and counted himself lucky he hadn't bitten his tongue.

"A-are you okay?" Roman asked, his fair eyebrows arching as he looked at Abraham. "Is *this* okay?" He gestured to himself. "If not, I can leave."

Abraham was trying to wrap his mind around this new—to him at least—version of Roman. He shook his head.

Roman recoiled, taking a step back, cheeks turning red. "Oh, I'll leave. I—"

Abraham hated that he couldn't reach out with his right hand to Roman then. "No, that's not—I was trying to shake myself out of…of—" He wasn't doing himself any favors with his bumbling explanation. Roman had taken another step back. "Don't leave," Abraham blurted out. "Please. Please don't leave."

All traces of uncertainty vanished from Roman's expression, and he smiled that shy smile that made Abraham's heart flutter.

"Okay. Can I come in then?" Roman asked.

Abraham had to swallow twice and give himself a stern, silent, *Get it together, dumbass* before he could answer. "Yes, please. Come in." He stepped aside and held the door open for Roman.

Seeing Roman wearing something other than shorts or ripped jeans was unusual. He looked good, very good, in his jeans and with his shirt tucked in, rather than how he usually wore it, which was untucked and therefore covering, or hiding, more of his body. His blond hair flowed down his back a few inches, the pale strands shiny and probably soft to the touch.

Abraham itched to touch it, to see if it was silky and warm. He kept his hands to himself. He wouldn't be groping Roman.

"This is a nice little apartment," Roman said a moment later, after Abraham had closed the door. Roman hadn't gone very far into it, but stopped a half dozen feet from Abraham, and was taking a slow look around. "I like the color scheme."

Abraham glanced about. The color scheme *was* nice. The blend of tan, green, dark gray and yellow worked surprisingly well. "I never would have thought to put those colors together. Always had white walls and brown furniture before."

Roman chuckled. The sound was almost musical, thought Abraham thought he detected a hint of nervousness.

"Roman," he said, waiting until Roman turned to him. "Why are you here?"

"Can't I come to visit?" Roman replied. "Other people do."

Abraham took a step forward. "Yeah, *other* people do, but until yesterday, you'd hardly spoken to me except for when we discussed your case."

Roman held up one finger. "I spoke to you the day you moved here."

"You did," Abraham agreed. "Though it seemed to me like you were uncomfortable at the time. Then yesterday, you sat by me." And it was confusing. "You didn't seem scared of me."

Roman flicked his glance down then back up to Abraham's. The apartment lighting was decent, and Abraham could see all the lovely flecks of colors in Roman's irises. He could also see the earnestness in Roman's expression as Roman moved closer to him.

"I'm not scared of you," Roman said, his voice quiet yet firm. "It's what I've always felt when I'm around you that made me nervous for so long. What I feel when I think about you."

Abraham couldn't be certain, but he thought Roman's lowered gaze was settled on his lips. Abraham licked them, and Roman inhaled, his nostrils flaring slightly.

"Roman," Abraham pled. "What are you doing here? Tell me. Make it clear so I don't misunderstand." There was absolutely no way he wanted to guess at what Roman wanted from him.

Roman came even closer, so close that he was only inches from Abraham. He looked up into Abraham's eyes.

Abraham's chest went tight and that buzzy, dizzy feeling returned. He couldn't be seeing what he thought he was seeing in Roman's expression. Roman couldn't want him. He was older, and weathered, and not anything special.

Except Roman raised his shaking hands up and cupped Abraham's face. For several heartbeats, they stood just like that, with Roman touching him, staring into his eyes, and Abraham letting him, opening himself up in some way he couldn't describe.

He felt exposed, his secrets laid bare, his infatuation and worry — his *love* — for Roman put on display.

And there was nothing he could do to stop it. Abraham wasn't even sure he *wanted* to stop it. He had carried his feelings for Roman for months, buried them so that he wouldn't scare Roman any more than he already had. "Whatever it is, Roman, anything… I'd… I'll do anything for you." The admission was torn from him, and it left his throat aching and raw, as if the words had been covered in sandpaper as they came up.

"This," Roman finally whispered, his eyelids lowering, head tipping up. "Do *this* for me."

Abraham didn't know what he meant, and before he could ask, Roman pushed onto his toes, while gently easing Abraham's face down. Abraham closed his eyes as their lips brushed together, a tender, chaste kiss that they held until Roman scooted closer, his body aligned with Abraham's.

Abraham's lips parted on a gasp, and he would have moved back had Roman not moaned. The sound was slight but unmistakable, and it rippled through Abraham. He dared to rest his left hand on Roman's hip, needing to hold on, to touch the man tearing him apart in the best way possible.

Roman moaned again. He was destroying Abraham's hesitation to ever do anything physically, together. Abraham would never have dared to make any sort of move on Roman, would never have thought Roman wanted him in return. But Roman was showing him with each close press of his body, with every bold glide of his tongue over Abraham's bottom lip, that he wanted what was happening between them.

Abraham parted his lips further, and bent down more so Roman didn't have to stay on his tiptoes. The reward was another moan from Roman, then the push of his tongue past Abraham's lips, into his mouth.

Yes, God, yes! Please, let him really want me. I want him, need him like he's the air I breathe. Abraham was almost desperate for Roman. A kiss had never turned Abraham on so much, but it wasn't just a physical arousal that was coursing through him. It was much deeper. His emotions had been laid bare. While he hadn't said he loved Roman, Abraham was certain it had been obvious.

He didn't worry about it. As Roman kissed him, sliding his tongue over Abraham's, and moved his hands down, one to Abraham's neck, the other to his left shoulder, all Abraham could do was give himself to Roman.

And Roman took, with a sweet touch that shattered Abraham's heart and rebuilt it at the same time. The innocence of the kiss was unmistakable, as was Roman's need. He pushed even closer, and the hard bulge of his erection pressed against Abraham's thigh.

Abraham trembled. Desire tangled his nerves, and made his legs weak. He swayed, then turned his head enough to break the kiss. "'M gonna fall over."

Roman hissed and slid his arms around Abraham. "I'm sorry."

It took Abraham a second or two to realize that Roman was hugging him—a full-body, strong-armed hug. "For what?" Abraham asked, running his left hand up from Roman's hip to the middle of his back. "Kissing me until I just about melted for you?"

Roman rubbed his cheek against Abraham's chest, and the endearing gesture made Abraham fall even more in love with the man.

"I made you weak in the knees?" Roman asked, glancing up at him.

That cute smile was leaning toward smug, and Abraham liked seeing Roman so confident. "You did."

Roman, beaming, moved around to Abraham's left side, then slipped an arm around his hips. "We can move to the couch? Or…" He gulped. "The bed?"

Abraham clenched his hand on Roman's back. "What's happening, Roman? How have we gone from you just beginning to speak to me, to this? To you offering…offering to…" He couldn't even get the words out.

"To wanting us to make love?" Roman finished for him, and *oh*, but he sounded so certain, his expression conveyed his sincerity as well. "To us wanting each other? Have you never felt desire for me?"

"Couch," Abraham stuttered, certain something in his brain had just shorted out. "I don't understand."

Roman led him to the couch. "Sit. You look stunned."

Abraham sat, turning as he did to keep an eye on Roman, who moved to sit in the chair by the end of the couch. "Of course I'm stunned." He didn't think he needed to repeat why.

Roman blushed but didn't look away from him. "Well, I… I get that. I mean, I know I've kind of stayed away from you, but it was because I felt things when I was around you, *good* things, just—I wasn't ready to deal with them. With wanting you."

"And now you are?" Abraham asked, rubbing at his left temple, where a dull throb had begun.

Roman leaned forward, his elbows braced on his knees, hands clasped together between them. "Abraham, I have had years to recover, to reach this point. I've had help—therapy, more than once, spiritual support, guidance, and time to heal. Taking this step, coming to you, should be proof to you that I want you, that I want to build something with you."

"Something as in what, exactly?" Abraham sighed. "Can you give me just a sec? I need to take something for this headache." He stood. "I'm trying to wean myself off the pain meds, and thinking now that maybe I should wait until the doctor tells me to stop them."

"You should." Roman stood as well. "Is your medicine still in the top drawer of the nightstand?"

Everything froze, or maybe it was just Abraham—there was a roar in his head, static and chaos, then silence as Roman stopped moving, stood, head down, one hand up as he'd been gesturing to the bedroom.

All Abraham could think was, *How did he know? How?* The weird vibes he'd gotten off and on around Miller, Gideon, and some of the other residents—most of the ones he had met—ramped up until he was nearly shivering. "What's going on, Roman?" Abraham rasped, heart pounding. He didn't like the direction his thoughts were taking. "How do you know where I keep my medication? Have you been in here when I'm gone?"

Roman turned around, shaking his head. "No! I've never been *in* in here before, not even before you moved here!"

"*In* in? What does that mean?" Abraham kept himself from snapping the question out. Even angry, he couldn't shout at Roman.

Roman came back over to him, and stared up at him. "You have to keep an open mind."

"I can do that." It was funny how he felt less alarmed, less inclined to be upset with Roman when he was so close.

Roman touched his chest, and Abraham felt it all the way to his heart. "Sit back down? You're hurting, and I don't like that. I'll get your medicine, and a glass of water for you, then explain—" He took a deep breath, then exhaled. "Well, everything."

"There's a bottle of water on the bedside table," Abraham said, then he sat down.

"I'll grab it." Roman rushed from the room but returned quickly. "Here." He handed over the prescription bottle and the water. "I guess I could have taken the pills out for you. I wasn't—"

"I can open it." The bottle had a flip top lid since Abraham couldn't do the press down and twist kind.

"Oh!" Roman sat on the coffee table right in front of him. "I didn't mean that you couldn't open it, just that I would have gotten the pills instead of the whole bottle, but I was trying to hurry."

Abraham took out two pills and set them in his right hand. He gave the bottle to Roman. "Thanks."

Roman flipped the cap then put the medicine on the table beside him.

After Abraham swallowed the pills, he leaned back, resting his head on the top of the couch cushion, and closed his eyes. "You know, I had a dream you were in here, a couple of times, actually. Is that creepy?"

"No, because I've dreamed about being in here," Roman replied. "Do you know what I do? My... My job, so to speak?"

"You make beautiful wooden bowls," Abraham said, picturing some of them. "Beautiful works of art. I want to buy all of them, but that seems unfair to the art world, so I'm waiting for the one that feels like it's mine. Plus, I figured you might think I was a stalker if I bought every bowl you made as soon as you put it out at the gallery."

Roman chuckled, and there was a rustle, then the couch dipped beside Abraham. He turned his head and opened his eyes enough to see that Roman had sat beside him.

"I don't think I'd have believed that of you," Roman said. "Not when I, more than you, know what's happening between us."

At that claim, Abraham sat up straight and couldn't repress a skeptical, "Is that so?"

Roman sucked on his bottom lip then let it slip from between his teeth.

Abraham wanted to kiss it. Hell, he wanted to kiss Roman until his toes curled.

"That's so," Roman said with utter certainty.

Abraham didn't want to doubt him, but he didn't see how that could be true. It was time for him to lay his cards on the table. "Roman, what's going on? I keep asking that, but I haven't gotten an answer yet. Please, explain it to me. What's happening with us? This town? There's something about this town, the people I've met. Y'all are kind of...clannish, maybe?"

"Not clannish," Roman denied, shaking his head. "I hate that word. I think you mean, we're more like a pack."

"Pack. Gideon said that yesterday, then tried to suffocate himself with a mouthful of burrito, and Miller gave him a dirty look," Abraham remembered. "There was definitely a weird vibe happening then."

"Because — okay, you're going to think I'm crazy, but I can prove this," Roman said. "We *are* a pack. We're coyote shifters — except for Iker. He's a wolf shifter. And Duff. He's human. Well, and Jess, Miller's mom? Her fiancé is human, too. But the Vonheimers aren't. At least not the ones we've ran into. They're mountain lion shifters. And I'm the medicine man for our pack. In training. Medicine man in training, though there's no one here to teach me. I'm learning through ancient texts and there's a shaman in South Texas who's been helping me, too."

Abraham's jaw had dropped open again, and he could only stare as Roman kept talking, or babbling, the words just spilling out of him. Disbelief and fear flared up but he stomped them down, determined to hear Roman out instead of listen to his own panicked thoughts.

"See, we lost the ability to shift some generations back," Roman was saying, flapping his hands as he talked, twitching at his shoulders and jostling one leg. He was very noticeably nervous. "So everyone was just kind of, well, human. I guess there were some people that had better senses, more acute senses, I mean, than others did. Sharper hearing, the scenting skills of a hound, or just about, things like that. Most of us were no different from anyone else, though. Then Gideon came along after he was kicked out of his bear clan — oh, he's a bear shifter, yeah — and he was Miller's prophesied bear and mate. Then some other things happened, and Miller found out that other shifters were losing the ability to shift too. We had to go back to the old ways. We'd forgotten our roots, our history, our deities. And in return, they abandoned us. But I haven't told Miller yet. I think there's more to it than just that. Not everyone can shift yet. I can't. I can't, and I'm the medicine man." He rolled his eyes, groaned, then slumped back. "So now that I've done this totally insane rambling-babble-athon, let me just add one more thing. I came here in spirit form, that's how I knew where your pills were. I had to see you, had to…to make sure you were okay and just be near you, but I wasn't ready to *be* with you. Astral projection, dream travel, whatever you want to call it. That's what I did, and that was intrusive, wasn't it? And wrong. It was wrong. Miller said I was a Peeping Tom."

"Roman." Abraham's headache hadn't ebbed at *all* after hearing all of that. The pain helped ground him, made him certain he wasn't dreaming. "Give me a few minutes, okay? You just… Jesus. You just told me more than I can process, and I'm trying not to flip out. It's a lot to take in."

"I can call Miller and Gideon, or just one of them, and they can show you," Roman offered. "They can shift. Or Iker and Gael, or most of the people you've met here. They can prove that I'm not making this stuff up. I promise, I'm not crazy."

Well, Roman might not be, but Abraham was feeling a tad unhinged.

"I won't say anything else until you're ready to talk," Roman added. He mimed locking his lips shut.

Abraham grunted, and flopped back, hoping his headache would dim somewhat so he could concentrate. He didn't even know where to start with everything he'd just been told.

Chapter Ten

Roman wanted to add one more thing—that he and Abraham were mates, but he'd promised to be quiet, so he had to honor that vow. Besides, he'd just had a major verbal overload episode. It probably hadn't helped Abraham's headache at all.

Texting Miller or anyone for that matter was out of the question since Roman had left his phone out in the car. After several minutes, his nervousness got the better of him, and he scooted a little closer to Abraham, who was still and silent, his head tipped back, tanned neck arched, Adam's apple bobbing on occasion, chest rising and falling steadily, except for the occasional hitch.

Another five minutes or so went by, and Roman moved closer again, his shoulder almost brushing Abraham's. He was on Abraham's left side, and Roman yearned to touch him so badly, his fingers twitched.

Roman edged closer, watching Abraham's face for any signs that this was not okay. He scooted closer still, until he was firmly pressed against Abraham's side.

Abraham grunted, and tugged his arm free from between them. He draped it over Roman's shoulders, and gave the slightest of nudges.

Roman took the offer up immediately, leaning against Abraham, resting his head on Abraham's shoulder.

And still, Abraham didn't speak.

Roman's cock had begun to harden as soon as he'd touched Abraham. Now it was painfully erect, pinched in his jeans, and he didn't want to squirm too much, but he had to make an adjustment down south or he was going to be miserable.

He repositioned his cock then noticed the steady, deep rise and fall of Abraham's chest, the slackness to his body, the heavy weight of his arm fully on Roman's shoulders. A soft, snuffling sound escaped Abraham's lips as he exhaled.

He's snoring – he's asleep! Roman wasn't upset. The medicine could have contributed to Abraham's need for a nap. That Abraham felt safe enough to sleep with him right there, after Roman's multiple confessions, meant the world to Roman. He didn't think even the medication could have knocked Abraham out if he'd deemed Roman untrustworthy or dangerous.

Roman pulled his knees up then curled into Abraham's side, his legs partially in Abraham's lap. He let himself relax, feel happy because he knew Abraham wasn't going to throw him out. Not Abraham, who was calm and steady, who had watched Roman for months with what Roman now knew was not quite-hidden affection and longing.

It felt right to be there with Abraham, snuggled close together. Eventually, Roman's erection softened, and he relaxed even more. He drifted for a while, not quite in the deep sleep stage, not awake all the way.

When Abraham's breathing changed, a hitch first alerting Roman to his impending awakening, Roman tilted his head back, lips parted, hoping, *hoping* –

Abraham tensed then sat up partially, looking down at Roman.

Then Roman tried his best to look seductive, lowering his eyelids, though that made it hard to actually *see* Abraham, and licking his bottom lip, scraping his teeth over it.

Abraham groaned, and slowly pulled Roman up, onto his lap. "Stop me if anything makes you uncomfortable," Abraham whispered, his voice rough.

Roman straddled Abraham's hips and buried his fingers in Abraham's thick black hair. "I'm fine, except I need to kiss you."

"Then kiss me," Abraham said. "Do whatever you want to with me."

Roman went hot with lust and affection. He raised up, his mouth almost touching Abraham's. "Whatever I want?"

Abraham grunted, and perhaps he'd intended to speak, but Roman pressed his lips to Abraham's and kissed him, less timidly than before, letting the hunger that was building in him free. He pushed his tongue into Abraham's mouth, tasting him again. The man had a flavor to him that Roman knew he'd come to crave.

Abraham moaned into the kiss, and cupped Roman's nape with his left hand.

Roman widened his knees, bringing his groin against Abraham's stomach. *Oh, gods...* It felt so good to move, to rub and rut, the friction to his dick good but not enough to get him off.

Roman whimpered and turned his head, trailing kisses down Abraham's chin, over his jaw, the prickle of stubble making him shiver. "I... I need—" He couldn't think to ask for what he needed. The chaotic arousal was pinging around from one nerve cluster to the next, and all he could do was feel.

Abraham hummed and arched his neck, giving Roman more skin to love on. He licked and sucked on parts of it all while writhing, snapping his hips faster. The press of Abraham's erection against his bottom every time Roman rocked down stimulated him even more. That he could make this strong, sexy man hard for him was an additional aphrodisiac piled onto Roman's already stoked-high desire.

"Want you," Roman muttered, nuzzling a sweet spot beneath Abraham's ear. He kept his right hand in Abraham's silky hair, but caressed every part of Abraham he could reach with his left.

Abraham's breathing had ramped up, becoming loud as he panted. He kept his hand in the middle of Roman's back, not moving it lower or higher.

"Touch me," Roman pleaded. "Touch me and make me come." Roman sat up and shoved his hands between them, unfastening his belt and pants in record time. "Abraham, *please!*" he begged when Abraham hesitated.

"'M not so good with my left hand," Abraham finally mumbled. "Kind of clumsy. But if you can get up on your knees…"

Roman started to ask why, but Abraham was sliding down, and Roman suddenly understood. He got his pants and briefs down enough to free his cock and balls, then he rose up on his knees.

"Roman, you're perfect." Abraham sighed. "Can I touch you?"

"Please!" Roman all but demanded, jutting his hips forward.

Abraham touched the tip of his dick, tracing over the slit. "Sweet man."

Roman shivered, then whimpered when Abraham took that finger, glistening with Roman's pre-cum, and licked it clean. "Oh my gods!"

Abraham's smile was nothing short of wicked while he sucked, then he popped that finger out of his mouth audibly. "Take what you want, Roman. I'm yours, shifter, shaman, anything you are, I'm with you."

"With me," Roman repeated, wanting desperately to thrust his cock into Abraham's mouth, yet holding himself back. "You believe me?"

Abraham looked him in the eyes. "I believe in you. That's all I know for sure."

Roman bent and kissed Abraham hungrily. He couldn't get enough of the man's taste, or the sounds he made, the sight of him—couldn't get enough of Abraham, period.

And it was incredible to feel so comfortable and turned on and *free*. *Only with Abraham, only ever Abraham.* Roman brushed his lips over Abraham's. "Only you," he repeated out loud. "Only you. My mate. My soul."

Abraham moaned, arched, and Roman couldn't wait any longer. He guided his cock to Abraham's mouth, rubbed the head over Abraham's swollen, wet lips. "Can I?" Roman asked.

Abraham licked over the tip, and Roman almost lost it then. "Oh!" He gripped his shaft, fisting the base and holding it hard. "I don't think I'm going to last long— Ah!" He thrust as Abraham sealed his lips around the crown, flicking his tongue over it as he sucked.

Roman tried not to just ram his cock in, but the velvety wet heat, the incredible suction, that talented, flicking tongue were combining to strip him of any self-control. He let go of his dick and pushed in deeper, gasping, shaking as pleasure swam through his veins.

He was aware of the feel of Abraham under his hands, warm skin, soft hair, hard muscles, the sounds he made while sucking, the moans and hums that vibrated along the length of Roman's cock.

Abraham kept that one hand flat on Roman's back, palm down, and he began to push, looking up at Roman, golden eyes gleaming.

Roman moaned and used one finger to trace Abraham's top lip, stretched around Roman's length. Then he gave in to Abraham's unspoken encouragement to thrust.

Pushing his cock slowly deeper into Abraham's mouth, Roman reveled in the gift he was being given, this sensuous treasure that was turning him inside out in the best way. Try as he might, Roman couldn't retain complete control of himself when Abraham swallowed around his shaft.

Roman cried out, the sound torn from him as his balls drew tight. He wanted to continue watching Abraham but couldn't keep his eyes open as he pulled his hips back until his cockhead dragged over Abraham's bottom lip, then thrust back in slowly, steadily, breaching Abraham's throat once again.

Nothing he'd ever done to himself felt half as good as having Abraham suck him. Roman kept moving, in, out, faster, until heat coiled in his groin. "Gotta—" he managed to grit out.

Abraham pressed harder on his back, making it clear that he wanted Roman's cum.

Roman gave in to his orgasm, letting ecstasy wrap around him, fill him, pour from his cock in hot jets of spunk.

Abraham sucked him through it, that hand at his back caressing instead of pushing.

When the passion and pleasure began to ebb, Roman whimpered as his shaft slipped from Abraham's lips. He sank down onto Abraham's lap. "So good," Roman whispered, eyes open, taking in Abraham's awed expression. Roman didn't know *why* Abraham was looking at him like that, but it made him want to kiss Abraham again, so he did.

The salty, bitter tang of his own seed on Abraham's tongue threatened to make his cock hard again. Roman pressed closer to Abraham, running his hands up Abraham's chest, a light touch that he hoped felt good.

Abraham moaned and kissed him back, canting his head to the left, giving them both a better angle.

The kiss was messy and perfect, and Roman didn't ever want it to end, but someone pounded on the door and startled them both.

Roman almost fell off Abraham's lap before he caught himself, slapping a hand on the back of the couch and grabbing a handful of it. "Expecting company?"

Abraham wiped his mouth off on his shirt sleeve. "Not that I can think of." His voice was gravelly.

"Is that—" Roman scooted off and began tucking his cock away. "Is your voice like that because of what we just did?"

"Deep-throating your cock?" Abraham asked, one eyebrow arching up and a smug look settling over his features.

"Yeah, deep-throating my dick," Roman agreed, not embarrassed or ashamed. He just didn't know what was crude and what wasn't when it came to the terminology.

"Yeah, and I loved every second of it." Abraham gestured to his own groin, and the wet spot there. "In case you couldn't tell."

"Oh." Roman started to reach down. "Can I?"

"You can do whatever you want with me," Abraham assured him.

The pounding on the door started up again. Roman growled. "Ugh. Not until whoever that is goes away, and they aren't going to do that until you answer." He eyed that wet spot again and grinned. "Well, maybe I should get the door, and you should go change."

Abraham winked at him—winked, and Roman nearly swooned, he was so surprised by the playful gesture.

"You've got a deal," Abraham said.

Roman helped him up while hollering, "Just a sec already!" He sent Abraham off to the bedroom, then did a quick self-check to make sure he was presentable before walking over to the door. He looked out the peephole and groaned. *Of course Miller and Gideon would show up now.*

Resigned to the impending inquisition, Roman opened the door and promptly blushed—possibly from head to toe—as both men smirked.

"You smell like sex," Gideon said brightly, a big grin obliterating the smirk. "High five!"

Chapter Eleven

Gideon was loud, and Abraham heard him all the way into the bathroom, where he'd gone instead of his bedroom. He had his sweat pants down and was wiping at the drying cum in his pubes, trying to clean up as fast as he could. Leaving Roman out there to be grilled or teased wasn't happening for long.

Abraham still didn't know what to make of everything Roman had told him, but the fact was, none of it was a deterrent. If it was real, then he'd find a way to believe it. Besides, there was something inside him that recognized the truth of Roman's words.

Maybe it had to do with his heritage, which he suspected was Native American, though he wasn't certain. One day he might have a genetic profile done just to find out.

He didn't dither over why he believed in Roman. He just did, and that was fine with him. For months, he'd wanted Roman—not just in a sexual way, and at first, not in that way at all. To protect Roman had been his first impulse, then the rest had come later.

Abraham kicked off his sweats. He hadn't bothered with underwear when he'd gone to bed last night, and had slept in what he'd been wearing when Roman had showed up. He found another pair of sweats in the hamper that didn't smell too bad and slid them on, then checked himself in the mirror. "Shit." Well, there'd be no hiding the purple love bites under his ear on one side, and near the base of his neck on the other.

He washed his hands and rinsed out his mouth. A quick run of the comb through his hair and he was done.

Abraham left the bathroom and strode quickly toward Roman. Standing in the living room, Roman, Miller and Gideon were speaking in hushed tones, but they all looked at him when he approached.

Abraham kept his stoic expression in place as he stopped beside Roman. He wanted to put his arm around him, but wouldn't make any move without knowing for sure it'd be okay.

Roman sighed and snuggled right up to him, slipping *his* arm around Abraham's waist. "They think you're going to freak out about everything, or that you don't believe me and are humoring me."

Abraham had to work hard not to glare at Miller and Gideon. "Why would I do that?"

"Because you're willing to tolerate his brand of crazy," Miller replied bluntly. "No offense, Ro. You know I don't think that."

Roman chuckled. "Well, yeah, because you're a shifter, and our alpha. Why would you think I made that part up?"

Miller rubbed the bridge of his nose, then turned and sat down on the couch. "That's not what I meant. I don't think you're crazy, period."

"What kind of man do you take me for?" Abraham asked Miller as Gideon grimaced and rolled his eyes. "I thought we were on the way to being friends, if not already there, and yet you think I'm the kind of son of a bitch that'd take advantage of someone who was mentally ill?"

"Way to put your foot in it, Miller," Gideon muttered. "Sheesh."

"That *is* pretty insulting," Roman agreed.

Miller set his hat on the coffee table. "Well, okay. I did screw that up, but it's hard to believe you'd just accept everything Ro told you without proof."

Abraham had two choices that he could see at that point. He could be mad and make this whole discussion more difficult, or he could remember that Miller had always been good to him, and was only worried about Roman.

He chose the latter. "Feels right to me."

Miller nodded. "Because you love him."

Roman gasped, then said, "Miller, that's not—"

"It's the truth," Abraham agreed before Roman could think it wasn't. Abraham looked into Roman's pretty eyes. "I've loved you for almost as long as I've known you. I just didn't know what to do about it, except try to protect you."

"Because of what happened to me?" Roman asked. "Is that why you didn't tell me?"

"Why would you want me?" Abraham twitched his right hand. "I'm older than you, and you're... God, Roman, you're gorgeous, you've got to know that. And now I'm half useless—"

"You are not!" Roman protested. "And age doesn't matter to me. We're both adults. You're my mate, Abraham. We're meant to be together."

Abraham turned to face Roman. "You said that, when we were—" He remembered there was an audience. "Being intimate." And he was pretty sure Gideon had just tried to smother a snort of laughter.

Roman nodded. "I did, because it's true. I felt it, here." He placed a hand over his heart. "Didn't you?"

Abraham had felt something from the get-go, that was for certain. "Yeah, and when you were telling me about the shifters, being a shifter, it didn't freak me out because I felt that there, too."

"Oh, that's because Ro thinks maybe you're one, too," Miller interjected. "Your parents aren't shifters, though."

Roman groaned. "I was going to get there, Miller."

Abraham was too busy trying to see if that felt right, but he couldn't tell. "Well, I'm adopted."

"That…explains a lot. Your parents were jerks, and you don't resemble them in looks or behavior." Miller cracked his knuckles. "Thank the gods."

"Have you traced your birth parents?" Roman asked.

"No way to. I was abandoned at a fire station when I was almost three. I don't have many memories from before then." Abraham had given up on trying to find out who his genetic parents were. They obviously hadn't wanted him. "Got some vague impressions, I guess, of a woman with black hair and a scar on her neck, and a man who looked like he was dying, he was so thin. Don't know if any of those are real or not."

"You couldn't tell the firemen or whoever found you anything?"

"No, I couldn't," Abraham replied to Roman's question. "I didn't speak until I was almost five."

Roman hugged him suddenly, and hugged him hard.

"Oomph." Hard enough to squeeze the breath right out of him, which kind of hurt, but Abraham would take it. He put his left hand on Roman's back. "Grandma insisted on my parents adopting me, and I don't know the story behind that. Just overheard them arguing one day, the three of them, and Grandma telling them that her making them adopt me was the one good and right thing she'd ever done. They didn't agree."

"How old were you then?" Roman asked.

"Twelve, but I'd already figured out Mother and Father didn't want me any more than my genetic parents had," Abraham explained. "Grandma wouldn't have left them anything had they not taken me, though. She said she wanted a grandson. Her son, my father—adopted father—was apparently sterile, but I don't think he wanted kids anyway. He just wanted his mom's money, and she tricked him into thinking he'd get it if they adopted me."

Roman frowned. "But she didn't."

"No, she did. She said she'd leave them her fortune, and that wasn't but about a half a million dollars. The rest of the money had been her late husband's, and it was *that* fortune which I inherited." Abraham pulled out of the embrace. "Let's sit. I'm worn out."

He led them to the chair, then sat down and patted his lap. "Or wherever you want to sit."

"This is fine." Roman sat on his lap. "Really fine."

"Okay, before you two get all tangled up in each other, let me just do this." Miller stood up and reached for the hem of his shirt.

"You don't have to," Abraham protested, though he *did* want to see what he thought Miller was offering.

"Me too." Gideon began by taking off his shoes. "I'm a bear. That might scare you, but don't worry. We retain our human faculties while shifted."

".Good to know." Abraham didn't watch the men strip. He looked at Roman instead, who twisted around until he had his back against the arm of the chair, and his bottom settled in the V of Abraham's thighs. "What kind of shifter might I be?"

"Hm. You could be a coyote, like me," Roman guessed. "I don't think you're a grizzly bear, but what do I know? If you're a mountain lion…"

When Roman didn't continue, Abraham remembered what he'd said. "I won't be. I won't be like them." *Like the Vonheimers. Mountain lion shifters.* "Maybe I'm not a shifter at all."

"We're ready." Miller cleared his throat. "And bare-assed naked."

Abraham looked over to where Miller and Gideon were standing, nude just as Miller had claimed.

Gideon had his hands over his belly. "Can we do it now? I hate people seeing me in the buff — except for Miller."

Miller grinned at him. "Yeah. Let's."

That was all the warning they gave before squatting.

Abraham was stunned — yet not — as he watched the two men shift, their human form bending and warping, hair sprouting out through their skin, bones and tendons making awful noises. It was over relatively quickly, and where Miller and Gideon had been, a coyote and bear — a very *big* bear — now sat.

"Still Miller and Gideon," Abraham murmured more for his own sake than anything else.

"Yeah, they are." Roman sat up, scooted to Abraham's knees, then stood. "I wish I could get my coyote out." He knelt and held out his hands.

Miller snorted, but Gideon lumbered over, his claws clicking on the floor with every step.

"Right, wouldn't want to be petted, Miller." Roman instead began scratching in front of Gideon's ears.

The sound Gideon made in reaction to that made Abraham laugh. "He's happy."

"Gid's a sweetheart," Roman said. "Miller thinks he's above being petted."

Miller stood up and shook from head to tail, then he loped over to Roman and yipped.

"Mm-hmm, I see how you are." Roman gave him some attention, too. "While they are still their human selves, they're also part animal. What feels good, feels good."

After another minute or so, Roman stood then sat with Abraham again.

Miller and Gideon shifted into human forms.

"You didn't freak out," Miller said after he'd gotten dressed. "So that's good. As a bonus, I have to tell you, Abraham, you definitely *are* a shifter."

"Yeah, I was gonna say that, too,' Gideon chimed in.

"How can you tell?" Abraham asked them, intrigued and excited about this new possibility.

"You smell like something wild," Miller answered. "So does Roman and every other shifter I've ever met, and here's the good part—while I don't know what kind of shifter you *are,* I know what kind you're not, and that's anything I've ever met, including mountain lions. Still, there was just this hint of something, I can't put my nose on it just yet."

"Can he shift with his arm and shoulder injured?" Gideon clapped a hand over his mouth. "Oopth."

Abraham wasn't offended. "That's a good question. A lame animal isn't going to live for long in the wild unless it heals up. This arm won't ever be the same. Anything I could turn into would be hindered more by this injury than I am now."

"Maybe," Miller conceded, "or it could be that when your abilities kick in, you might find yourself healing up a bit more than you would otherwise. We'll just have to wait and see."

"Okay. Now, about this mate business," Abraham began, focusing on Roman. "What does that mean?"

"It means what I said. I'm yours, you're mine, we won't want anyone else," Roman explained. "It means that I love you, too, and know you're the man who completes me."

"Just that fast?"

Roman scowled at him. "It wasn't fast. We've known each other for *months* and it took me *forever* to catch on to what I was feeling for you. Once I started to believe it, I knew I wanted you, and that meant working for it. I wasn't ready, and I might still have some...some issues."

"I'll be there with you, or I'll step back, if that's what you need," Abraham promised. "Anything. You can count on me." Then he asked, "You really love me?"

"Oh yeah," Roman said, smiling at him. "I do."

"I can't believe you'd want a beat-up old guy like me," Abraham started. "Well, older than you."

"You're perfect for me." Roman cuddled right in against him. "But I want you to live with me, if you will. Stay with me at the ceremonial hall? Please?"

"We're gonna leave you two to discuss your plans, but if you need help moving anything, holler at us." Miller put his hat on then tipped it at them. "See y'all—Oh, there's a pack meeting tomorrow night that you're invited to, Abraham. In case Ro hasn't mentioned it yet."

"They were probably kind of *busy*," Gideon all but sang as he followed Miller to the door.

"Don't want to think about that," Miller grumbled. "He's like my kid."

They left the apartment, and Roman got up again. "Well, that was fun. I'm locking the door, then...*then* can we go to your bedroom?"

Abraham wasn't telling him no again. "We can go anywhere you want to."

Chapter Twelve

Abraham sat on the edge of the bed as Roman asked him to.

"Can I touch you?" Roman asked. "All over?"

Abraham's cock went from zero to sixty in a matter of seconds as he nodded. "Anything. Just like I said before."

"Are you afraid to touch me?" Roman stepped up between his legs. "Afraid I'll freak out?"

He couldn't lie to Roman. "I don't know. Will you?"

Roman hitched one shoulder up in a lazy shrug. "You aren't them, Abraham. I don't think I'll slip into a place where I ever think you are. I've had a lot of sessions with my online therapist regarding sex, and she thinks I am capable of moving past what happened. I would like you to move past it, too."

"As long as you promise me you'll speak up if I do something that makes you uncomfortable, or that you don't like," Abraham said. "But I really would like to let you have your way with me—whatever that way might be. Despite being older and bigger, I'm not particularly toppy, though I can switch."

Roman placed one hand on Abraham's chest. "I'm glad you told me that." Then he pushed, not very hard, just enough that Abraham got the message. He lay back.

Roman traced the center of Abraham's torso, all the way down to the waistband of his sweats. "I should have had you take the shirt off."

Getting in and out of the loose sweatshirt with one hand was hard enough when he was upright. "I can't do it lying down."

"You don't need to do it at all." Roman climbed up on the bed and began pushing the shirt up. "Oh, look at that. Yum."

"Yum?"

"Treasure trail," Roman explained. "Nice and dark, but not super thick. Mm, and you have abs, just a little fuzz on your stomach. I want to see more."

Roman began kissing Abraham's belly—soft butterfly kisses and longer, sucking ones.

Abraham touched Roman in return, caressing his shoulder and back. He'd never hated being injured more than he did then, when he couldn't use both hands like he wanted to. He was able to move his right arm some, but holding it up for more than a few seconds wasn't possible.

He soon stopped worrying about his inability to move it much when Roman delved his tongue into Abraham's belly button. At the same time, he slipped one hand beneath the waistband of Abraham's sweats.

"Please, touch me," Abraham begged without shame, parting his legs further. Roman was on Abraham's left side, and as he lightly traced the length of Abraham's cock with one hand, he found Abraham's nipple with his other and began to brush his fingertips over it.

Abraham moaned and writhed, showing Roman how much he liked what he was doing. He wanted his clothes off, wanted to be naked and exposed, vulnerable and laid bare for Roman. Abraham wanted that so badly a whine escaped him, and he'd never made such a sound before.

"Abraham," Roman murmured, his breath warm against Abraham's belly. Roman sat up and moved off the bed. "Time to get undressed." He stepped between Abraham's legs, then grabbed the waistband of his sweats. "Butt up, honey."

Honey. Abraham had been called a lot of things in his life, but never an endearment, not that he could remember. It went straight to his heart. "Love..." He wasn't sure what he'd intended to say, lost his words when he met Roman's heated gaze.

Roman tugged. Abraham raised his hips, and the sweats slipped down, Roman whipping them off before dropping them on the floor.

"Gods, you're gorgeous." He licked his lips as he stared at Abraham's cock. "You'll have to tell me what to do, if I mess up. Don't be shy. Tell me so I can learn what pleases you best."

"You. You please me, Roman," Abraham told him.

Roman placed his hands on Abraham's knees, and slowly inched them up his thighs. "I'm glad, but you know what I mean. I've never done this. I've never been with someone, had sex with someone. I don't want to do it wrong." He stopped with hands at the juncture of Abraham's thighs and groin, his thumbs just brushing Abraham's balls. "Teach me how to love you."

Abraham's heart did a slow *lub-thub* as emotion washed over him. Love, affection, joy and desire all warmed him as he wiggled his hips. "Right now, anything you do is going to feel amazing, but if you mean what to do when you're sucking me, just... Keep your teeth covered." Abraham showed him how, only feeling a little goofy.

Roman nodded. "Got it. And if I want to explore first?"

"Let me get this shirt off?" Abraham asked.

"I'll help." Roman took Abraham's left hand and half-tugged him upright. "I just want to touch you everywhere."

"You can," Abraham said. "Face, chest, dick, balls, ass, armpits, legs — anywhere you want to touch me, fuck me, anything you want."

Roman's shaky exhalation was followed by him grabbing the bottom of Abraham's sweatshirt and lifting it up. He took it off and tossed it down. "I want to play, and see what makes us both get off."

Abraham smiled and cupped Roman's chin. "I'm all yours." The idea of Roman, in all his innocence and curiosity, exploring him, with him, was mind-bogglingly hot.

Roman nipped at Abraham's hand, then crawled right into his lap and kissed him. There was nothing tentative about the kiss, no gentle prodding or nervousness. Roman began a sensual siege and laid claim to Abraham's mouth, and Abraham shivered, wrapping his left arm around Roman's hips, hand resting just above the swell of Roman's ass.

With Roman clothed and him not, Abraham felt deliciously raunchy, more exposed than he ever had before.

Roman sucked on his tongue and Abraham forgot to breathe. Then Roman moved, was out of his lap and tracing the scars on Abraham's chest instead.

"I'm sorry you were hurt," Roman murmured. He bent and kissed the worst of the scars, where surgery and infection had left the skin puckered and permanently swollen, the tissue thick. "I'm glad you didn't die. I had a vision of you, watching yourself from above."

"It happened, more than once," Abraham confirmed, goosebumps pebbling his skin all over as Roman continued the sweet kisses. "I had to come back. Couldn't—couldn't leave you."

"Don't." Roman stood up, and this time it was he who cupped Abraham's chin. "Don't leave me, ever." Then he kissed Abraham again, the hard press of lips almost bruising.

Abraham all but came then and there. He grabbed a handful of Roman's butt, jeans and all, and moaned, humping against air since Roman wasn't close enough to him.

Roman growled, and that sound fired Abraham's cock up even more, pre-cum leaking from the slit.

Then Roman moved away again. "On the bed, in the middle, give me everything."

Abraham scrambled back, clumsy instead of graceful like he wished to be, but he got the job done, collapsing onto his back, spreading his legs wide.

"Bend your knees," Roman suggested. "I want to see everything."

Abraham had never put himself on display. He'd had a few hook-ups over the years, one boyfriend that had lasted six months or so, and almost every time he'd had sex, it'd been him taking control. To give it up was intoxicating.

He bent his legs, dragging his heels almost up to his ass, clenching it as Roman watched. "You want to fuck me?" Abraham asked. "You can."

Roman stripped off his own clothes but didn't answer. He walked around to the foot of the bed while

Abraham held himself still and simply admired the beauty of Roman's form, the slender torso and legs, pale skin, white-blond pubic hair framing his long cock. Roman's nipples were tiny, dark circles, the tips of which were already erect. He had deep hollows above his collarbone, and a slight swell of Adam's apple, not the more protuberant kind like Abraham's.

There were no scars marring his smooth skin, not on the front, at least.

Abraham could never be half as beautiful, half as perfect, but he was fine with that. He was what Roman wanted, *who* he wanted. Who he loved.

"Fucking, you said," Roman surprised him with.

Abraham frowned. "Yes?"

"Is it fucking?" Roman got on the bed, kneeling. "I never understood if that was a crude term or not. Is all making love fucking? Is fucking ever making love? Because when I think of making love, to me, it'd be a slow, sensual experience. Fucking implies less time spent on the details. But that's just my opinion."

Abraham's face heated as he said, "I guess making love is one of those phrases I think of other people using. Never thought there'd be any love in the sex I had, but I was wrong. I don't think the words matter so much as the actions and intent, the emotions. If you fuck me, that doesn't mean we aren't making love."

Roman nodded. "Okay. I don't think I'm ready for that. I'd like to touch you—" He blushed all the way down to his chest. "Your asshole. Can I?"

Abraham clenched it and his cock bobbed as his lust surged higher. "Hell yeah. I don't have any lube, but get your fingers wet enough, and that'll do."

"It won't hurt?" Roman asked, a worried expression flickering over his face.

"No. I'll tell you if anything hurts," Abraham promised him. "I will. Please, just…" He pressed his lips together, unwilling to push Roman in any way.

Roman knee-walked forward then sat between Abraham's feet. "Can I do this?" He palmed Abraham's sac. "Oh, wow, that feels nothing like holding my own."

Abraham got a strangled, "Yes," out as he shifted his feet, trying to get them further apart. He settled for pulling his knees to his chest, offering Roman his ass, his balls, his cock.

"Sexy," Roman said, giving Abraham's balls a gentle squeeze. "So big. Your cock, too."

Abraham's cock was a little longer than average, but Roman had him beat in length.

"I like the way this arches." Roman bent and licked a path up from the base of Abraham's dick to the underside of the crown.

"Please, suck me," Abraham begged. "Unless you don't want— Fuck!"

He couldn't keep quiet as Roman lipped the bundle of nerves under his cockhead, stimulating Abraham almost unbearably. It took every ounce of his control not to reach down and try to jack off left-handed, which never worked well for him.

Roman murmured something against that sensitive skin, then licked it, and Abraham arched, crying out Roman's name.

Then Roman sealed his lips around that spot and sucked while rolling Abraham's balls with one hand, and reaching up to pluck at his left nipple with the other.

Pleasure streaked from Abraham's chest to his ass and all points in between. His fingers and toes tingled and he closed his eyes as he struggled not to come so quickly. He hadn't been an early shooter before today, but weeks of being unable or uninterested in getting off, combined with months of wanting Roman, were flipping all his control switches off.

Roman plucked at Abraham's nipple and licked the tip of his cock.

Abraham let his legs fall open again, heels digging into the bedding as he tried to keep from thrusting.

"Sweet," Roman said. He gave Abraham's nipple a pinch, then brought that hand down to fist Abraham's dick. "Love this." He opened his mouth wide and sucked on the tip.

Abraham loved it too. He moaned and shook — great, full-body tremors that felt like an aerobic workout. When Roman took another inch into his mouth, and nudged Abraham's balls up, it was all Abraham could do not to shout the walls down.

Though he did shout, a wordless sound that left his throat aching. Roman did something that caused vibrations around Abraham's dick — laughed, hummed, whatever it was, it was amazing.

Roman moved his hand up and down Abraham's shaft while sucking harder. He was a noisy lover, which only served to turn Abraham on even more. He loved the messiness of sex done right, the slurps and spit, cum and sweat, sore muscles, satiation and exhaustion. He loved Roman, and the things Roman was doing to him — jacking, sucking, moving that other hand down until he was tracing over Abraham's asshole.

Abraham ached to move, to thrust, and he had to, just a little. He also wiggled his butt down, trying to encourage Roman to put a finger in him, even dry.

But Roman didn't. He just rubbed over and over Abraham's pucker while sucking his cock until Abraham wanted to scream in frustration, to beg for more. Which he did. "Please, please, Roman! Put your fingers in me, fuck me with them until I can't... I can't—" He didn't know what he'd meant to say, because Roman slid his mouth off Abraham's cock, and down, down, over his balls, giving each a lick, then further, beyond them to the patch of skin underneath, and—

"Roll over," Roman ordered, his voice husky. "I want to try something."

Abraham was *all* for what Roman wanted to try. He flipped over in record time, and arched his back, sticking his ass up in a silent plea. But he also grabbed a pillow and tossed it back.

"Yeah, this will help." Roman tapped Abraham's ass. "Up."

Abraham curled his hips up, and Roman put the pillow under him.

"You have a gorgeous butt," Roman said. "I would have thought it'd been hard, muscular, but you've got padding that makes it just right."

"Padding." Abraham chuckled despite his intense arousal. "Got a fat ass, you mean."

"Not fat." Roman caressed it, then squeezed each cheek. "Perfect. Plump, and just what I want to bury my face in."

Which was all the warning Roman gave him before parting Abraham's buttocks and licking down his crease.

Abraham's strangled shout when Roman tongued his hole was followed by a curse as Roman pushed his cheeks farther apart and began rimming him with unmistakable enjoyment. Unmistakable, because Roman's moans were louder than his own.

Roman kneaded Abraham's butt while licking and kissing his hole, pressing his tongue against it, flicking, gliding, until the tip penetrated Abraham.

Abraham just about lost his mind. He started to come onto his knees, then did so as Roman pulled and tugged him into that position.

Roman hadn't exaggerated about what he wanted to do. He pressed his face into Abraham's crack, rubbed and licked and loved on him until Abraham's dick steadily dripped pre-cum.

Only then did Roman push a finger into him, slowly, both of them panting. "Gods, you're so tight inside, and hot, hot—" Roman kissed one ass cheek, then his balls before moving up to lip at the skin above his hole.

Abraham was useless—all he could do was moan and shake, and rock back in tiny increments, though he tried to stay still.

The second finger burned in a delicious way as Roman worked it into him.

"Where is it?" Roman asked. He wiggled his fingers.

Abraham jolted then slammed his hips back despite his best attempts not to. Pleasure spiraled up from inside his ass to every nerve cell in his body. The bright, spinning currents of bliss stole his breath and his pulse roared in his ears.

Then Roman reached around and gripped Abraham's cock. He spread the pre-cum around and began to jack him firmly while fingering his ass.

Abraham lasted an embarrassingly short amount of time. He tried to hold back the orgasm tightening his groin, drawing his balls up. Clenching his muscles backfired. Ecstasy burst in his bloodstream like tiny invaders, spreading in rapturous ripples as he climaxed.

Roman finger-fucked and jacked him through it, nipping Abraham's ass a couple of times, which made Abraham shudder and call out Roman's name.

Abraham's strength left him when his orgasm ebbed, and he eased his butt down, Roman's fingers slipping from his hole.

Roman pulled his other hand out from beneath Abraham's hips. "I want to rub off on you."

Abraham grunted, "Yes," and wished he had the energy to open his eyes, and mirrors hanging from the walls and ceiling so he could watch Roman get off.

Roman straddled his ass. "This okay?" He pressed his cock between Abraham's cheeks. "I'm gonna use your cum for lube, gonna just—" He thrust. "Oh! Oh, yeah."

The dirtiness of it all, of Roman taking Abraham's spunk, spreading it on his own cock, then rubbing it into Abraham's crack while getting off was a fantasy come true, one Abraham had thought of before, but it'd never felt as good as it did in reality.

Roman thrust hard against Abraham's ass. The sound of their bodies meeting was loud in the room, almost as loud as their breaths.

Then Roman growled again, fucking Abraham's crease faster, rougher. He worked one hand under Abraham's hip and just held on.

Abraham clenched his ass, and Roman growled a third time. The sound was amazing, strong, and as wild as Roman.

"Love you," Roman gasped. "Abra—Abraham!"

A hard shove, then Roman stilled and hot cum splattered on Abraham's lower back. Roman pumped again, and more seed spilled onto Abraham's skin. He felt two more spurts before Roman began to slide off of him.

Or so Abraham thought. Instead of moving away from him, Roman began to lick at the semen puddled on Abraham's back.

Abraham's eyes shot open, and his cock tried valiantly to harden.

Roman laughed and licked him again.

Abraham liked the sound of that laughter, as if Roman was already coming up with something devious to do with him. Abraham liked it a lot.

Chapter Thirteen

Moving Abraham in with him would have gone a lot smoother if everyone would have just given them some space. But that wasn't how the pack worked

Roman opened the door to let his mother and sister in. They'd both met Abraham before, during the investigation. They hadn't met him as Roman's mate.

Miranda, for once, didn't say anything snarky to him. She surprised him with a hug. "Congrats!"

The Apocalypse must be nigh... He hugged her back. "Hey. Abraham will be out of the bedroom in a minute or two. He's just making sure everything is packed up." *Or hiding, because we're being invaded by well-wishers.* The Fervent Five had showed up half an hour earlier, right after Miller, Gideon, Gael, Iker and Gideon

Roman cast Miller a mock-glare. This is what he got for texting Miller and letting him know Abraham was moving into the ceremonial hall with him. At least he and Abraham had had a good twenty-four hours alone until then.

Gael came out of the kitchen. "There wasn't much food to pack up."

"I was just going to ask you if Duff would want it." The human had been homeless and one of Gael's only friends on the streets in El Paso. While Roman rarely saw Duff, he did care about the man's health. "He doesn't leave his apartment much."

"I worry that he's become agoraphobic," Iker said. "Or he's just afraid that if he leaves, he won't have a home to come back to. We're trying to get him to agree to visiting us, but he doesn't even like to come next door. It's getting pretty bad."

"What about online help?" Roman suggested. "It helped me. I can give you my psychiatrist's name, or I can talk to Duff, if you think that'd help. He's kind of one of our pack, isn't he?"

"He doesn't know about us. What we are," Gael added, gesturing to himself and Iker. "None of us, I mean. I'm not sure he can handle knowing."

"I could approach him as a friend. I'd like to be that to him." Roman wanted to fulfill his duties as medicine man. He *needed* to. At times he doubted his calling, but for the most part, the desire to serve his pack was strong and growing more so every day. With his mate beside him, Roman felt more secure and stronger than he had in the past.

"I'm not certain how he'd handle that, but maybe you could go over with us sometime next week, once y'all are settled," Gael suggested.

"Sure. I'd be happy to." Roman saw Abraham coming down the hallway, a small duffle in hand. "Is that everything?"

"There's not much," Abraham replied. "Oh, hello, Lilith, Miranda."

Lilith went right up to Abraham, framed his face in her hands, and planted a big, smacking kiss on his lips. "Welcome to the family and the pack, Abraham!"

"Thank you." Abraham's ruddy cheeks just made Roman want to kiss him...all over. "I appreciate that, ma'am."

"No ma'am stuff," Lilith warned, patting Abraham's arm. "I'm old enough to be your mom, so it's that or Lilith."

Abraham frowned. "You don't look old enough to be my mom."

She smiled brightly. "Well, I like you even more for saying that, but I *am* fifty-six. Started having my babies in my thirties."

"Wow. You look incredible," Abraham said.

Lilith lit up with pleasure and gave him another kiss before walking over to talk to Miranda.

"There's nothing left to pack." Abraham held the duffle up. "Nothing much here was mine in the first place."

"Maybe you didn't think so, but Miller and the rest of the pack gave you everything in here. All the furnishings and decorations." Roman pointed to one bare wall. "We've got rooms in the hall we can put things in. The building is sectioned off. Ceremonies are held in the center, or outside behind it if the ceremony calls for being outside. Living and guest quarters, kitchen, bath, all of that is there behind the center of the hall and to the sides. We've got plenty of room."

"I need to thank a lot of people, it seems," Abraham said. "I didn't know these were my things."

"Yes, and if there's anything there, Gideon's arranged to have some of the pack go get anything in your apartment in El Paso in a few days."

Abraham shook his head. "Nah, that's not necessary. My clothes and stuff that was there had been ripped to shreds. I didn't have anything else there, really. My laptop is here. TV didn't matter to me. Nothing personal. It was just a place to sleep."

"Okay, then we're ready, I guess." Roman slipped his hand into Abraham's. "Let's go home."

The day was overcast with the threat of rain and thunderstorms on the wind. Roman could smell it, and a current of electricity that ran through him warned of potentially severe weather. He looked up at the sky as dark clouds rolled overhead. "This looks like a bad one coming in."

"Yeah, we'll probably be under tornado warning in a bit," Miller agreed. "So let's get this stuff moved, pronto."

The ceremonial hall was outside of the town of Del Rey, but not far. Fifteen minutes later, Abraham was holding open doors and Roman was advising people on where to put what.

Thunder cracked and the hall shook. Roman wasn't the only one that startled. Several people shrieked in surprise.

"Gods, that was a loud one," Roman observed, one hand to his chest. "I like storms, but the thunder startles me."

Abraham glanced around them, then whispered, "Bad storms make me nervous. Seen a tornado pick up a couple of cars and toss them around when I was first on patrol as a police officer in Sabinal. Was just luck it wasn't my cruiser that got picked up. There were no survivors in those cars."

Roman wound his arms around Abraham's hips. "That's awful. I've seen a couple of tornados forming but never one close up. I don't want to, either." He snuggled against Abraham. "So you were a cop in Sabinal?"

Abraham slipped his left arm around Roman. "Have to be in law enforcement for at least eight years before you can become a Texas Ranger. Sabinal is where I started out," he explained, rubbing his cheek against the top of Roman's head. "Then, once I was a Ranger, I was stationed out of El Paso. That's how I ended up here, working your case."

"Destiny," Roman murmured.

"Yes." Abraham's simple agreement was followed by another burst of thunder. "We'd better get everyone either settled in here, or off to their homes."

"Sounds like hunkering down here is the better idea." Roman sighed. "I wanted more alone time with you, but we'll have to wait. How about a mini-packed lunch instead? We've got plenty of stuff for sandwiches, and bags of potato chips."

"That'll work." Abraham smiled. "Then we'll have each other alone tonight, and the things you're going to want to do with me...hmmm."

Roman untucked his shirt. It'd do little to hide his erection, but it was the best he could do at the moment. "Help me get everyone together after we set up for lunch?"

"Sure." Abraham stiffened as another round of thunder shook the building. "I don't like this. I'm trying not to freak out, but—I know people make comments about me being stoic. They've never seen me in a bad storm."

"We'll be all right." Roman didn't feel any kind of danger, but that didn't mean anything. He hadn't had a warning of the attack from the Vonheimers, after all. "Come on, we'll stick together, and if you need a break, we'll go to our room. I want to give you a proper tour of it, and the rest of the building, at some point."

Once Roman told Miller that lunch would be ready soon, Miller and Gideon set about getting everyone together. Rain had started pouring down in sheets, and while no one was forced to stay, no one wanted to leave, either.

Abraham would tense every time it thundered, but as lunch progressed, and everyone talked and laughed, he seemed to relax some. Roman tried to keep one hand on Abraham at all times, for both of their sakes. He liked touching Abraham—he'd never guessed how sensual he'd be once he found his mate.

Roman wanted to be naked with Abraham as much as possible. They were so perfectly matched when it came to sex. Granted, they'd only been together for one day, but Roman didn't think that meant he was wrong.

In the middle of the night, when he'd been rubbing his cum over Abraham's nipples, Abraham had begged him not to stop. He let Roman explore and play, and had encouraged him to do both, actually. Roman wanted to drag Abraham right down the hall to their bedroom…not that he'd have to drag Abraham. He'd go willingly.

"Where's your mind, son?"

Roman blinked and realized his mother had just asked him a question.

"Yeah," Gideon chimed in. "Where's your mind? You look kind of sweaty, Ro."

"Sweaty?" Roman touched his forehead. It was dry.

Gideon smirked. "I meant flushed."

"I don't think I want to know where his mind went," Miranda said.

He was tempted to tell them all exactly what he'd been thinking, just to shut them up and make them stop teasing him. Before he could bother, thunder rolled again, and the lights flickered out. He felt Abraham's thigh stiffen under his hand. Roman leaned over and rested his head on Abraham's left shoulder. "We'll be fine," he whispered while the others chattered.

He'd barely gotten the words out before several alarms went off, cell phones chiming a warning.

"Tornado warning," Lilith said over all the racket. "We should take cover."

"In the hallway, or —" Miller was cut off by a sudden, great roaring sound, much like a train bearing down on them from outside. "Run for the hallway and cover your heads!"

Roman leaped up with Abraham beside him. It was dark, but several people had the flashlights on their phones on.

"Out, out, out!" Miller bellowed. "Hurry!"

Roman and Abraham were bringing up the rear of the group. As they reached the doorway, a terrible shrieking and shaking overtook the building, or at least their part of it.

Abraham shoved him, pushing Roman out into the hall. "Get down!"

Roman reached for Abraham and found him — Abraham tackled him, and together they hit the floor, Abraham taking the brunt of the fall but rolling Roman under him.

Roman couldn't even protest. He knew Abraham was protecting him, that it was in Abraham's nature to put his life on the line for others. He'd never have been a Texas Ranger otherwise.

But he was going to chew his ass over risking his life once this was over.

The walls and floor shook, then a rending sound was followed by debris raining down around them. Roman heard the *pings* and *plonks* along with louder noises, that roaring making his ears ring. The wind buffeted them violently, and he held onto Abraham's left arm, which was tucked under him. Roman reached back with his right hand and cupped Abraham's head, doing what he could to protect him.

And Roman believed, with every fiber of his being, they would survive this.

Chapter Fourteen

"We'll have to rebuild it all." Miller sighed and dusted off his hands.

Like everyone else there, he was a mess.

Abraham was thankful everyone had survived the tornado with only scratches and bruises to show for it. The building was, as Miller pointed out, more destroyed than not.

Abraham watched Roman a few feet away, tending to Miranda's scrapes. "We were lucky. I hate tornados. This is the second one I've been entirely too close to, but we're all okay. Just dinged up. This"—he gestured around them—"it's just a building. Granted, I get that it's a sacred spot. It can be rebuilt and consecrated or whatever it takes to make it sacred again."

"Yeah, I imagine it can. Roman will have to look into that." Miller sighed. "Just, damn. It's been a rough few months. And you look like you're hurting."

Abraham's arm and shoulder were throbbing, not that he was going to admit as much. "I'm fine."

"You are not," Roman snapped, coming right up to him. "You're holding yourself like you're in pain. Where were your pain meds?"

Abraham didn't argue. He pointed toward the back of the building, which was now in ruins. "That way. Kyra took the bag with them in it to our bedroom."

"Damn it." Roman huffed, looking up at the remains of the ceiling. "We need to get out of here. This isn't a stable roof. I want to check the nursery first, though. There are some plants I had that can be used to help you. Did any of the vehicles survive the tornado?"

"Paul went to check, but I didn't see any of them close by. At least, not where we left them," Frisky added. "They could be on the other side of this wall, for all I know."

"We're lucky we didn't have a truck dropped on us." Gideon scowled. "I like Texas a hell of a lot less than I did an hour ago. What kind of crazy shit is that? We were having lunch, then the world goes crazy."

"Mother Nature at her finest, Gid," Miller told him. "She's beautiful and fierce, deadly and unpredictable. All the technology in the world can't change that."

Gideon folded his arms over his chest. "You're way more admiring than I am."

"Miller, your truck is the only one that didn't get sent flying," Paul announced, running up to them. "Sorry, all the rest of us are screwed. There's car parts strewn all over out there, and most of our vehicles look like they've been through a compactor."

"Ugh. I *just* got that Jeep," Brandt muttered.

"Hey, we're all alive and relatively unharmed," Roman pointed out.

Brandt shook his head. "I'm only alive until my dad finds out I missed the insurance payment on the Jeep."

"Ouch. You dumbass," Kyra said. "I wouldn't blame your dad for burying you with the Jeep, but he won't. He'll just lecture you, then work double shifts at the refinery if he has to in order to pay the Jeep off."

"No, he won't," Miller interjected. "Brandt is going to pay his own debts."

Brandt nodded. "Right. How am I gonna do that?"

"Work at the gas station," Miller snapped. "I'm not joking. You can't hang around with your friends and goof off anymore. You did something stupid, and you're going to fix it."

Abraham hadn't seen Miller like that before—bossy, assertive, and commanding respect. Not a single person could look him in the eyes. Abraham didn't try—he was busy watching everyone else. He definitely picked up on Miller's alpha vibes, yet felt no need to avert his gaze or to challenge him. It was something for Abraham to think on and discuss with Roman later.

"Yes, alpha," Brandt said with obvious respect. "I will. Won't. I mean, I will about the job part, and won't keep goofing around."

"Thanks for ruining the Fervent Five," Tandy snapped at Brandt. "Now we're actually *all* going to have to grow up!"

"We can hang around the gas station," Paul offered.

"No," Kyra countered. "Miller's right. We've all stuck together like we can't live for more than a few minutes apart. Even at night, we usually sleep over at one of our houses. What are we so afraid of?"

"We'll discuss this later. Right now, vacating the premises seems like the best plan." Miller pointed to the door. "Out."

Outside, the drone of engines could be heard. "Reinforcements?" Abraham wondered. "Pack coming to see if everyone's okay?"

"ATVs, and probably," Roman said. "Cell towers aren't working so no one could text or call."

The debris outside was considerable. Trees, shrubs, pieces of lumber and tin, trash cans and other things Abraham didn't have the chance to examine were strewn all over. Rain was still falling, albeit more of a drizzle, and the wind was gusty. The sky was dark gray with patches of white, and lightning zipped across it after thunder boomed.

Abraham would have considered moving somewhere that didn't have tornados, but he loved Texas, and Roman, and he was growing fond of the pack. That meant he was staying put, and he needed to learn to cope with his fears about tornados — although he didn't think those fears were unreasonable.

Roman tugged on his arm. "By the way, if you ever put your life before mine again, I'm going to be very angry. It's not that I don't appreciate it."

"Shit." Abraham wanted to kick himself. "Did I—"
How do I ask?

Roman turned and glared at him. "I *told* you, you don't remind me in any way, shape or form of the assholes that raped me. Stop it."

Hearing Roman say it, to bluntly speak of his rape without fear or cringing, only increased Abraham's admiration for him. He'd known many rape victims who hadn't been able to get that word out, and he understood it. Every one of those people, and Roman as well, were stronger than he'd ever be. Abraham didn't know if he'd be able to keep his mind together if he'd gone through what they had.

And Roman clearly meant what he'd said, adding, "It's an insult to me at this point. I have worked very hard to get past what happened. I will never forget it, and I won't be the man I would have been had it not happened, but I am *not* broken anymore. I just have some cracks, but who doesn't?"

There was no need for Abraham to answer the rhetorical question. He did owe Roman an apology. "I'm sorry."

Roman's glare turned to that sweet smile that turned Abraham's insides jittery. "I get that you're a protector, but when it comes to you, and my pack, so am I."

"I'll remember that." Abraham winced as the pain in his shoulder throbbed hotter for a couple of heartbeats.

"I should check the nursery," Roman began.

Miller cut him off. "It's gone. Look."

'Gone' was right. There wasn't a plant left in sight, and the nursery itself was little more than twisted metal, glass and concrete.

"You can get your prescription refilled at the Del Rey Pharmacy on Main, can't he, Miller?" Roman asked.

"Yeah, Larry owns it, and he's one of us," Miller replied. "Assuming the pharmacy is still there. I don't know which way the tornado went or how long it lasted."

"Is that...?" Abraham nodded to the east, toward Del Rey. "Is that smoke?"

"Smoke?" Roman repeated. He and Miller, along with Gideon and Jess, stared as an inky spiral slipped up into the sky.

"Shit!" Miller exclaimed. "That is definitely smoke!"

Miller took off running to his truck with Gideon beside him. "Y'all wait here for the ATVs."

"I'm coming with you!" Jess hollered, and she joined them in the truck before Miller put it in drive and left.

"I don't like the direction of that smoke," Roman murmured, still staring at it. "The apartments lie that way."

Abraham's gut cramped. "Gael and Iker are here, but Duff—"

"Is there," Roman finished.

It seemed to take hours for help to arrive. Abraham knew some of the people on the ATVs, though none very well.

"Where's the smoke coming from?" he asked Eddie, who he'd met before at the gallery months ago.

Eddie shrugged. "Dunno. Wasn't anything burning when we set out, least not that I know of."

That seemed to be the general consensus amongst the newcomers.

Abraham glanced back at the remains of the building behind them. One area seemed completely undamaged, right by the destroyed nursery, and the hall was intact, for the most part. Other walls were still erect here and there. Overall, though, he didn't see how there could be much of anything salvageable left. He turned back to his Roman. "Are you okay? Not physically—I know you aren't hurt—but you just lost possibly everything."

Roman shook his head. "I've got you, and everyone I care about, and my office looks like it was completely skipped over, which is miraculous I think. Also very strange. In that room is every book I have about our kind, and it could have been scattered all over, for anyone to see, or gone forever."

The idea of which gave Abraham a chill. "We're clearing it out?"

"As soon as we can," Roman agreed. "I want you to have your medication refilled, then we'll come back here and load up everything we can. I'm not comfortable leaving any of those texts behind."

"We can do that first," Abraham said. "Stay here if we need to, and someone can go get my SUV or someone

138

else's. You never know if something might short out and start a fire or what have you."

Roman looked like he wanted to argue. He didn't. "Eddie, can you see if Larry will refill Abraham's pain meds? They were somewhere in this." He thumbed over his shoulder. "We want to stay here until someone can bring an SUV or a truck with enough room for my things from the office. Maybe the rain will let up by then."

"One of us can stay here," Paul offered. "We don't mind."

"No, go to town, get dry and see if anyone in town needs help," Roman said. "We're worried that the fire is at the apartments."

Eddie nodded. "Might be. It's the right direction for it." He cupped his mouth. "Everyone going back to Del Rey, find someone to ride with! We're heading out!"

"We'll be back with the medicine for Abraham," Kyra promised. "The Fervent Five aren't abandoning post, just running out for supplies."

"They're a good group," Abraham said after they'd left him and Roman behind. "Pack. I meant they're a good pack."

"The best," Roman replied.

"It's funny. When Miller was handing down orders, I noticed that everyone kind of bowed their heads, or at least averted their gaze from him. I could feel the power coming off of him. I understand that's because he's the pack alpha."

Roman made an approving sound, almost a hum. "Then what seemed funny about it?"

"Not funny, I guess, just strange in that I didn't feel the least bit intimidated or anything," Abraham confessed. "I wasn't irked by him being the boss, but I wasn't inclined to think of him as such, either. Doesn't mean I don't respect him, just that he didn't *feel* like he was my leader, I guess. It's hard to explain."

"Hm. Maybe it has to do with what kind of shifter you are. I don't know." Roman swiped at his hair, which was dripping wet. "Do you think we could stand under the eave by the office, if we can't go in there?"

"Why can't we go in? It's the only place that looks stable." Abraham would check it out first—as he was sure Roman would do. "Getting out of the rain sounds great."

Chapter Fifteen

"Here they come. I hear a vehicle coming." Roman handed Abraham his laptop. "I'm glad everything in here was fine."

Abraham added the laptop to the box on the desk. "Tornados are like that. They're powerful, but they can take one room and leave the next, one house and not the other, one car…" He shook his head. "I think maybe this being a sacred place helped, though. There's not even a hint of damage to this room or the roof."

"I agree. We do need to figure out what to do in case of future risks to these books. I'm transcribing one now, but there's so many of them, it'd take me years to do them all." Roman picked up the box. Abraham took what he could with his left hand. "The rain *did* stop, right?"

"Hasn't been hitting the tin roof, and the skies were more blue than not last time I looked outside, but let me double check." He had to set the books he'd held back on the desk. He opened the office door and looked. "All clear."

"Thanks." Roman went outside. Abraham followed.

Paul and the rest of the Fervent Five approached in two SUVs. Neither of them were Abraham's, which made sense.

"We didn't even think about your keys," Roman said. "Where are they?"

"On the key ring with the ones to the apartment, in my pocket." Abraham chuckled. "Not one of my brighter moments."

Roman noted that the white lines that framed Abraham's mouth when he was hurting were more pronounced. So were the wrinkles at the outer edges of his eyes. "You need to take something and lie down for a while, and I feel like I'm ready to collapse."

"A nap wouldn't hurt either of us," Abraham said.

Paul parked the blue SUV and Kyra parked the red one. They got out, and Brandt, Frisky and Tandy joined them.

"The apartments got struck by lightning," Kyra said, her eyes huge. "We got your medicine—"

"Duff? Is he okay?" Roman demanded.

"We don't know. No one can find him. Miller and six others are trying to track him, but…but your Tahoe is gone." Kyra took the books from Abraham. "The theory is, he hotwired it and left when the fire started."

Abraham winced as he rubbed his chest. "I don't want to call it in and report the Tahoe as stolen, but I might be able to pull in a favor or two and have some officers on the lookout for it unofficially. I just hope he's okay."

Brandt held his arms out to Roman. "I'll take that. The fire took out all the apartments on the right end of the complex."

Roman inhaled sharply. "Duff, Gael, Iker, and Abraham's apartments are all gone?"

Brandt nodded. "Yeah. Well there's parts of them still there, and a couple of other apartments are done for, but that's about it. Miller's trailer got ripped away, too. Going to have to be some pack rebuilding done here quick."

That was the most Roman had heard from Brandt in possibly ever. "Duff must have been scared."

"And now his home is gone. I hate that it happened to him," Abraham said. "To Gael and Iker, too, but Duff sounded like he really needed that safe place, and now it's gone. Shit, he can keep the Tahoe just as long as we can make sure he's okay, and I'll tell him that myself."

"He can't afford the gas," Roman countered. "Better we find him and give him another home. Maybe one built of brick."

"And we need a cement-walled one for your office." Abraham sighed when Kyra brought him two pills.

"I read the label. I hope that's okay." She had a bottle of water in her other hand.

"It's fine, thanks." Abraham took his meds and gulped down the water after Kyra gave it to him. "We should get to town and help wherever we can. Naps can wait."

As much as Roman wanted to claim otherwise, he didn't. Abraham was right. The pack, and the people of Del Rey, needed to come together and help each other.

* * * *

"It's frustrating," Roman said hours later, pacing the motel room. His mother had offered up his old bedroom, but Roman had wanted more privacy. The Motel 6 wasn't fancy, but it *was* clean, and there was no Miranda or Mom banging on the door.

Abraham sat on the bed, his back against the headboard. "Yeah, it is, but you have to be patient. It's one thing you learn being a cop, or a Ranger. Rushing can get you or someone else killed. I'm not saying that's the case with finding Duff, but he might panic if cops came after him. I don't know him so couldn't say."

Roman stopped at the side of the bed. "How's your shoulder and chest?"

"Hurts a lot less," Abraham answered. "I still think I should have rescheduled tomorrow's PT—"

"No, you're going, and I'm driving, and we will only be gone a few hours," Roman reasoned, burying his nervousness about driving in El Paso. With the town of Del Rey sustaining so much damage, the people and pack needed everyone available to pitch in. Miller and Gideon were more essential than Roman was. "We'll meet up with Jack, Jess's fiancé, and bring back supplies. Maybe Del Rey will get some kind of disaster funding."

Abraham cleared his throat. "I, ah. I could help, financially."

"We're talking millions, Abraham," Roman pointed out. "Even if you have many millions, you shouldn't spend them all here."

Abraham held out his hand to Roman. "I do, actually, have many millions, and I inherit another ten plus interest on my fortieth birthday. Money isn't going to run out."

Roman felt dizzy as he reached for Abraham's hand. "You're really that rich?"

"More money than I'll ever need," Abraham agreed. "It never felt like mine. Instead, I viewed it as the spoils of a hateful war between my grandmother and parents."

"Your childhood must have been awful." Roman let himself be drawn down onto the bed, where he sat facing Abraham. "Was it, or did you have good times, too?"

"It wasn't all bad," Abraham said. "My grandmother was kind to me. I think she loved me in her own way, though I don't know why. I don't know why it was *me* she insisted on having her son adopt. She could have bought them a womb and a blond-haired baby, you know?"

"She never told you?" Roman asked.

"Not a word about it. I only heard her and my parents arguing like I mentioned before," Abraham replied. "My father—and I use the term loosely—told her he would have adopted a baby that at least had a chance of resembling him or his wife, and my grandmother told him she didn't care about looks, it was about what's inside that—" Abraham's eyes widened. "Do you think she knew?"

Roman scratched his chin, thinking it over. "I don't know how. I mean, unless your genetic parents were shifters with the ability to still shift? And she saw them, or knew them?"

Abraham turned a ghastly shade of gray. "I remember her talking about how her husband was a big game hunter until he was killed. That was the same year I was adopted."

"Oh gods." Roman imagined some horrifying scenarios. "She didn't leave behind a journal or anything?"

"That'd be neat and easy, but no. She wasn't a writer," Abraham said. "She was good to me up to a point. I always thought if she'd *really* loved me, she would have adopted me herself, or wouldn't have left me with my adopted parents all the time, or with the nannies. Once, when I was going to college for my criminal justice degree, she said something that made me think her husband had been abusive. She told me to watch out for women who smiled all the time, as in, make sure they were safe. Those smiles could hide a world of pain, and abuse happened across all financial levels. She had become a big supporter of feminism and a frequent anti-domestic abuse donor. I wish I'd have asked her, but we weren't that kind of family."

"So we may never know the truth about your genetic family, though maybe you'll shift soon. We'll still be having the ceremony tomorrow night. It's the second full moon this month—a blue moon, which means a powerful one." Roman reached out and stroked Abraham's taut belly. "Some of the blue moon ceremonies get very…sexual. No children are allowed to attend." He could feel the heat of Abraham's body through the T-shirt.

"Yeah? Sexual as in, what?" Abraham's belly rippled, and he gripped the hem of his shirt. "Are we talking orgy level sexual?"

"Sometimes," Roman admitted. "Not mated pairs. They don't stray, but if two or three or a dozen adults decide they want to fuck, no one stops them. Sex is powerful magic, anyway."

"Is it?" Abraham sat up and Roman helped him get the shirt off. "So are we about to make some magic?"

It was a corny line, but Roman laughed, charmed by his mate. "Yeah, we are. You know what else was in the bag with your meds?"

Abraham leaned back again. "No, what?"

Roman's dick began to harden. "Lube. Nice of our friends, eh?"

"Oh, yeah, very nice." Abraham put his hand on top of Romans, and moved it down, closer to the growing bulge of Abraham's cock. "You going to fuck me, baby?"

"Maybe, or I might just suck you until you scream and come down my throat, then…the possibilities are endless, aren't they?" Roman closed his hand over Abraham's shaft and squeezed.

"Um, that feels so good." Abraham closed his eyes and thrust his hips. "Everything you do to me feels amazing."

"I want to taste you again," Roman told him. "You know I don't have much experience, but what we've done together so far has been more than enough. We don't have to have anal sex if it's not something you really want."

"I want, but only if you do," Abraham said. "It's been a long, long time since I've bottomed. Years, and the idea of that fat dick of yours spreading me open—fuck." He shivered. "Mm, yeah, I'd love that."

Roman began pulling down Abraham's sweats. "Then we'll get there, but for now, want to taste you. You taste so, *so* good." He had to get up to get Abraham's sweats off all the way, and to shed his own clothes. Roman did both quickly as Abraham began fondling his own dick.

"That's so fucking sexy." Roman groaned. He climbed back on the bed, straddled Abraham's thighs then fitted his mouth to Abraham's.

At the same time, he reached behind Abraham with one hand, finding his cock, and with the other, he went right for a nipple. Abraham shuddered and wiggled. The hard, wet drag of Abraham's dick in Roman's hand was incredibly erotic.

Roman sucked on Abraham's tongue and pinched his nipple while jacking him slowly. Abraham had let go of his own shaft and instead clutched at Roman's arm, then he tweaked Roman's right nipple, and Roman almost came unglued. He jerked his head back and demanded, "Again!"

"Anything," Abraham rasped, giving it another pinch.

Fiery tendrils of need burst throughout Roman's body. He kissed Abraham again, and thrust his aching dick against his stomach.

Abraham whimpered, the sound stimulating Roman even more as he swallowed it down. He needed everything Abraham would give him. Another pinch to his nipple and Roman was too close to coming. There was so much he wanted to do, and that meant he needed to gather his shredded control up and hold it tight.

To that end, Roman slid off Abraham's legs, releasing his cock as he moved. "Roll over for me. You loved it when I rimmed you yesterday, and I loved doing it." *A lot.* Driving Abraham crazy like that was fantastic.

"You don't have to, but if you insist—" Abraham practically climbed up him, trying to roll over.

Roman laughed and moved out of the way. "You need to be rimmed every day."

"Mm, no one ever bothered until you, but every day makes me seem greedy." Abraham peered back over his left shoulder and winked. "Every other day, maybe?"

"Eventually, but until for now, I'm thinking daily. And nightly." Roman gripped Abraham's ass and spread his cheeks. "Sweet, honey. Perfect." He dipped his fingertips into Abraham's crack. "Tell me what you want more."

"Anything," Abraham rasped. "As long as you're touching me."

Roman moved his hand down until his fingers brushed over Abraham's tight, hot little pucker. *What would it feel like to slide my dick inside of him here, to feel his inner walls rippling around it?* Roman bit his bottom lip to keep from begging. He traced over that opening again, then gave it a good, firm rub.

Abraham jerked his head to the side and cursed as he pressed his butt back. "Fuck, fuck me with...with something!"

Roman bent so he could kiss and nibble Abraham's buttocks while he rubbed his fingers in circles over Abraham's asshole.

"Roman, I need..." Abraham gasped and rutted against the bed, his hard cock getting a workout.

Roman wanted to crow with pride every time Abraham moaned or writhed. He wanted to push a finger into Abraham's ass, but not without some sort of lube.

"Be right back," Roman said by way of explanation. "Lube. I need the lube."

"Hurry, please," Abraham begged.

"I am." Roman ran for the bathroom, where the bag from the pharmacy was on the counter. He grabbed the tube from it, then rushed back to the bed, leaping and making Abraham bounce when he landed.

Both of them laughed, Roman giggling more than anything as he popped the cap open. "Argh! It has foil—" He twisted the lid off and poured the viscous liquid into his palm, sloshing it over the sides of his hand and down onto his legs and the bedding. "Oops." He used his chin to pop the top closed, then he moved right back behind Abraham and, with his clean hand, pressed one of Abraham's ass cheeks aside.

Then he went to town on Abraham's ass, licking, kissing, even nibbling gently at it, laving the puckered skin until that little muscle started to relax. When it did, once Roman could push his tongue right inside, he brought his dripping fingers up, still slick with lube, and slid two into Abraham's opening, watching eagerly as they glided in easily, more easily than they had the day before.

And Abraham loved it, calling out Roman's name, gasping, keening, rocking his hips until he was slamming back, taking Roman's fingers in fast and hard.

Roman found Abraham's prostate, more by luck than skill, same as before, and he massaged it mercilessly, pushing more of those hungry, pleasure-filled sounds from Abraham.

Then Abraham arched his neck, tendons in it standing out, and he shoved his left hand under his belly as he turned his head to the side.

His inner walls clenched and pulsed around Roman's fingers, harder every time.

Roman watched Abraham fall apart for him, watched him come, studied the lines of his back, the divot of his spine, the winged cuts of his shoulder blades, the scar above the right one, the parted lips, pants slipping past them, Abraham's eyes closed tight as he came and came.

When Abraham's hole unclenched, Roman eased his fingers out. "You are stunning," he whispered. "The gods couldn't have created a more perfect man. Give me just a minute." Roman got up, went to the bathroom, and washed his hands. He brushed his teeth, then returned to Abraham, now lying on his back, eyes still closed, a pleased, sappy expression in place.

"I just want you, all of you," Roman said, not even certain what he meant by it. "And you said, I can have you."

"Always," Abraham whispered.

Roman sat on the bed beside Abraham. He spotted the lube and put it by Abraham's hip. "So many plans." Roman bent and kissed him.

Abraham moaned softly, burying his left hand in Roman's hair, caressing, not holding him in place. He tasted every bit of Abraham's mouth, learned his flavor all over again, and which spots made him shiver.

Then he left another set of purple love marks down Abraham's neck and on his chest, all the way to Abraham's left nipple. Roman lapped at that little thing right away.

"So good," Abraham babbled. "Warm—oh yeah, please suck it more!"

As if Roman would ever refuse such need. He loved and sucked on that tip while gently rubbing the other. Then he switched, keeping his weight off Abraham's chest, not wanting to cause him pain.

But he needed more, too, had to come eventually, so he eased down onto his knees between Abraham's legs, leaving more kisses and nibbles, tugging at Abraham's treasure trail with his teeth.

"You—" Abraham cleared his throat. "Never had anyone make me feel as good as you do. Not nearly as good." He spread his legs. "I—"

Whatever he'd intended to say was cut short either by his own will or by the feel of Roman mouthing his balls.

Abraham's strangled sound was followed by him burying his hand in Roman's hair again. Roman rubbed his face up, down, and all over Abraham's balls. He inhaled, smelling Abraham there in that intimate spot, reveling in the scent of his musk.

Abraham's balls were big, heavy, hanging low. Roman loved them. He sucked one, then the other before opening his mouth wide and sucking the entire sac into his mouth.

"God! Roman!" Abraham yelped, curling up, abs rippling, tight.

Roman released Abraham's balls, then ducked his head down and pushed up on Abraham's right leg. Abraham raised it and Roman murmured his gratitude before he licked Abraham's burgeoning erection from base to tip and back down again.

Abraham grunted, spreading his legs even further apart as he flopped back. His balls drew up close to his body.

Roman's own nuts were aching. He ignored them in favor of cupping Abraham's while mouthing his way up Abraham's dick again. Several nice, fat veins ran up it, and Roman was fascinated by the feel of them under his tongue. He moved up without hesitating and sucked the crown past his lips.

Abraham shouted, thrusting the smallest bit. "Sorry, sorry! I didn't mean—"

Roman growled and gripped the base of Abraham's cock, which shut him up immediately. Next Roman tongued the slit, tasting the faint salt of pre-cum. He did it again, and again, until Abraham was gasping his name.

Then Roman sucked his cock in deep, as deep as he could take it. He couldn't handle it breaching his throat, but he enjoyed getting a good mouthful of Abraham's dick—enjoyed it so much that he could have sucked it all night.

In fact, he loved everything about giving Abraham head, from the bitter, salt and brine flavor, to the spongy, hard yet velvety texture of cock. Add in the sounds slipping from Abraham's lips, the desperate, small thrusts as he struggled to maintain some control, while Roman pushed him further and further away from it, and Roman could have sucked him for hours if his jaw would let him.

Roman brought his other hand around to Abraham's ass and immediately sought out his hole again. It was still slick with lube. He pressed two fingers in, slowly at first, then he pulled them out and thrust back in harder.

He kept sucking Abraham's dick, using his tongue to flick and rub along the underside. He'd intended to maybe fuck Abraham this time, but what he was doing was too good to stop. He couldn't stop fingering Abraham's pucker, caressing his gland every time he could manage it.

"Gonna… Fuck, I've gotta—" Abraham gasped, writhing, those sweet inner muscles contracting around Roman's fingers.

Roman jacked the lower part of Abraham's cock while sucking him faster. He wanted Abraham's cum on his tongue, hot and salty. Roman's mouth watered in anticipation.

Then he felt it, the swell of the shaft followed by the spurt of liquid. Simultaneously, Abraham's ass clamped down tight on Roman's fingers.

Roman tried to swallow every drop of the bitter load, unwilling to waste any of it. He reached for his own cock, intending to stroke himself to a quick release.

Before Roman got his hand around his shaft, Abraham sat up and pushed him onto his back. Roman caught himself on his hands. "What are you gonna do with me?"

With the way his cock thrust out, it was in perfect position for Abraham's wet, hot mouth.

"Fuck!" Roman fell back as Abraham took his shaft down to the base. At the same time, Abraham rubbed over Roman's balls. Roman keened as he fought back his orgasm. It was a fruitless attempt—he had little restraint against such overwhelming pleasure, especially when Abraham hummed around his shaft. That quickly, Roman was overwhelmed by the intensity of his climax.

He must have shouted, must have screamed and cursed and called out Abraham's name, because after he came and came and came, his throat ached and he could hardly swallow.

Abraham sucked until Roman whimpered, his cock too sensitive to take any more stimulation, even the velvety caress of Abraham's tongue.

Roman opened his eyes and watched in lazy satiation as Abraham moved up to kiss him. The taste of his own spunk almost made Roman's cock rise again, but sleep was tugging at him, exhaustion weighing him down, even there.

They kissed until Roman was floating on a pleasant cloud of contentedness. The horrible day topped with the fierce lovemaking was taking its toll on them both, and Roman wrapped his arms around Abraham and let his worries go.

Chapter Sixteen

Miller poked at what had been the couch in Duff's apartment. "We don't really have a fire inspector. There's a volunteer fire department the next town over, you saw 'em yesterday, but they're short-handed. I don't think anyone's going to be able to tell us if this fire was started by lightning or what."

"You don't think it was?" Abraham asked, tensing. His PT had gone well, but he'd wanted to get back to Del Rey. So had Roman, and in what little daylight they had left, both were going over the burnt remnants of the apartments that had been destroyed.

"I don't know, and that's the problem," Miller said. "You had a Vonheimer in your place in El Paso. Then this happens, and your Tahoe's gone, and Duff's missing—that's a lot of coincidences to me. Now." He stood up and fisted his hands on his hips. "I'm not saying it couldn't all *be* a coincidence, but where's the Vonheimer, and the other one that got away after they attacked us and shot you, huh? Why was one at your apartment? You know as well as I do, nothing good's coming from that. Unless he tore your shit up to help teach you a lesson about not clinging to material things." Miller snorted and rolled his eyes. "Aw, shit. I ain't doing that eye-rolling crap. I'm not fifteen, and even when I was, my mom would have smacked the back of my head hard enough to knock my eyes out for giving her that kinda roll."

Abraham chuckled, but he didn't feel the least bit happy. "What do we do, then? I can hire someone to come out here—"

"So can I," Miller cut in, eyes narrowed. "Don't start throwing your money around."

Abraham held up his hand in a placating gesture. "Don't snap at me for wanting to help. I'd like to bring in some jobs, build some houses out here. Maybe even set up one of those tiny house communities, but with a storm shelter nearby. One of those cement rooms, and Roman needs one, too. Stop scowling and tell me why I shouldn't help a community—a *pack*—that I'm a part of."

Roman moved to stand beside him. "Miller, seriously."

Miller sighed. "God damn, I'm just stressed. I'm worried, and we have the blue moon ceremony tonight. Our pack needs that after yesterday. No one died, but mine wasn't the only home lost, and this, these apartments, weren't the only business hit. Most of the damages are to shifters, because there's a hell of a lot more of us here than humans, but we're gonna help everyone."

"And I want to pitch in," Abraham argued. "It's not like I can do much physically, now, can I? So money, that I can give plenty of."

"It's my damned ego, ain't it?" Miller rubbed the back of his neck. "Yeah, I reckon it is. Why don't me, you, and our mates sit down with Mom and Jack—he'll be helping us with figuring out how to legally do things, and what the costs will be—tomorrow night?"

"Okay, and Miller? Thanks." Abraham awkwardly offered his left hand to shake.

Miller used it to pull him into a hug. "Man, I don't know what you are, but it ain't scared of me at all, is it?"

"Nope," Abraham agreed. "But I also don't want to challenge you or piss on Roman's leg to mark my territory. I'm assuming those are good things."

Roman giggled and Miller laughed. "Yeah," Miller said. "No pissing on Ro. If y'all like those kinds of games, I don't ever, *ever* want to know about it."

"What kind of games? Are we talking kinky sex games?" Gideon asked as he trotted over from where he'd been talking to Kyra and a few other people. "Because no. That's not allowed."

"And it wasn't happening. Abraham was basically letting me know he wasn't feeling like an alpha, but he also doesn't feel like he's gotta be lower down on the rungs in the pack," Miller clarified.

Gideon wrinkled his nose. "Well, yeah, that's not fun talk either." Then he grinned at Abraham. "We can rule out you being any kind of wolf or coyote. Or coywolf, have you heard of those? I wonder if there'll be shifters. Too bad our only coyote-wolf mated pair are both guys. I mean, that's not too bad— Aw, screw it. Y'all know what I meant."

"Yeah, but it's fun to listen to you babble," Roman teased. "Feel free to go on about the coywolf thing. Iker and Gael just pulled up."

Gideon mimed zipping his lips. "No way. I already put my foot in it."

Roman grinned. "You know you shouldn't have zipped your lips if you were going to keep talking."

"I couldn't zip them anyway. How often have you seen me be quiet when there's a joke to be made or a way to embarrass myself?" Gideon asked.

"You aren't that bad. Everyone loves you." Roman high-fived Gideon. "Now, Abraham and I have to go back to the gallery and look through the books y'all are holding for me. Abraham was right about needing a safe place for them. What if they ever were stolen, and humans found out about us? Most of the texts just refer to the responsibilities of shamans and medicine men, but there's a couple that mention us as a species."

Miller pointed at Abraham. "Get on with having a safe place for those built. No arguing from me."

"Will do." Abraham and Roman said goodbye to the others, then walked the few blocks to the gallery.

Inside, Miranda was behind the counter. "Hey, how bad was it?" she asked.

"Four apartments are completely demolished, another two have some damage. The rest are okay," Roman told her. "Are you here alone?"

"Just for a few minutes. Rudy went to get us some Ding Dongs. I have a craving for them, and he does, too." Miranda tilted her head slightly. "Why? You think it's dangerous for me to be here alone?"

Roman cast a quick glance his way.

Abraham didn't know what had happened between Roman and Miranda, but he understood their relationship had changed recently and Roman wasn't sure how to handle it. Abraham helped his mate out. "It's probably best for everyone to pair up at the very least."

Miranda waved him off. "Oh, no one ever looks at me twice. I went away to college and I swear I was invisible on campus. It's better here, but I'm just not going to be drawing anyone's attention."

"Hey, Ran, you know you're beautiful," Roman said, and Abraham could hear the nervousness in his voice.

Miranda looked startled. "That's sweet of you to say after I was so awful to you for so long. Let me tell you what I learned when I wasn't here anymore, though, Roman. I learned that it doesn't matter what you look like on the outside, when it's just you, all that's important is what you're made of inside. I was a jerk, and jealous, and immature, and I hurt you." She sniffled and swiped at her eyes. "And I promised myself that I'd do this alone, just you and me, but you're here, and you were kind after I've been cruel."

"No, no don't—" Roman ran over to Miranda and pulled her into a hug. "I forgive you. I wasn't exactly pleasant, either."

Miranda sobbed and clung to him. "No, no don't apologize. You were just a kid, and those men did awful things, and I was jealous because Mom paid so much attention to you! That's all on me."

It sounded like it *was* all on her, but Abraham stayed quiet. He wondered what had made Miranda have such a change of heart, and some of the possibilities made him feel ill. He'd have to find a way to broach the matter with Miller, and maybe even Roman.

The door opened, the bell on it chiming. Abraham turned to see Rudy coming in with a paper bag.

Rudy stopped, gaze on Roman and Miranda. "Oh, were they fighting again? I thought they'd chilled "

"They have chilled and gotten over it," Abraham explained. "Now they're going to get along just fine."

Rudy nodded. "That's good. Want a Ding Dong? You know, the chocolate cupcake-like things? I've got some Sno-Balls too, if you'd rather have marshmallow and coconut with your chocolate?"

"No, thanks though." Abraham didn't need a sugar hit. "What time are y'all locking up?"

"In about an hour," Rudy said. "They're done hugging it out. I'm going in with the sweets. Wish me luck."

Abraham assumed Rudy was joking as he walked right over to Miranda and started chatting, taking items out of the bag. Miranda might have missed the besotted looks Rudy was giving her, but Abraham didn't. Miranda wasn't as invisible as she believed herself to be.

Roman came back to him. "Sorry. We had a moment, though, and it was good." He wiped at his cheeks, which were damp here and there where he'd missed some tears. "Really good. I'm glad that happened."

"Me, too. Here, let me." Abraham brushed the wet spots off with his fingertips. "Now, what do we need to do to get ready for tonight?"

* * * *

As the moon rose overhead, more pack members came to the newly cleared ceremonial field. There'd been debris that had had to be moved, but several members had taken care of that. Now Roman was setting up small altars around the edges of the circle where people were gathering. Each altar held three metal bowls with incense burning in them.

Abraham had helped Roman cleanse the area with sage, and the scent of it still clung to them both. Moving around the circle, chanting with Roman, waving the bundle of dried sage as it slowly burned, had felt natural and right to Abraham. He thought he'd found his calling—helping Roman in his duties as medicine man. Abraham didn't have any urge to *be* a medicine man. He was content serving at Roman's side.

When the moon was centered overhead, Roman stripped out of his clothes, all the way down to nothing. Abraham followed suit, as did every shifter there, including Miller and Gideon. It should have been uncomfortable for Abraham, but with every second, the ceremony and the moonlight seemed to flow directly into his soul.

Roman took hold of Abraham's left hand, held it and started chanting.

Abraham didn't know the words. He tried to follow along and ended up humming more than anything else. Slowly, a warm, comforting sensation began to roll through him, and he'd have sworn it passed from his hand to Roman's.

The chanting sped up, and a strange sense of power seemed to thrum in the air. It grew with every word, and soon the place was thick with tension that was, to Abraham at least, a sexual one.

Roman raised their joined hands up in the air, and the wind picked up, wicking sweat from Abraham's skin. His cock rose, hard, eager, and he began to lose the ability to focus on anything but the need to tangle his body with Roman's to be taken, and take in return.

Then the chanting stopped and the silence was too loud. It lasted only a moment before a low moan sounded.

Abraham opened his eyes, not realizing he'd even closed them. His brain was stuck in neutral, but his body was all about sex.

Even so, he turned to Roman, and knelt before him. Let Roman decide what to do, if anything, because Abraham wouldn't push, though begging wasn't out of the question. He'd never needed anyone more than he needed Roman to fuck him then.

Chapter Seventeen

The heat from Abraham's body, the way he knelt, patient but so obviously filled with lust, combined to send a message straight to Roman's already erect dick.

The primitive part of him that grunted in response to fear, that made him want to bare his teeth and bite while he was making love to Abraham, pushed to the forefront of his being. He reached for Abraham, wanting him to stand up again. The wild, animalistic urges trying to take over Roman's body both thrilled and scared him.

"Give in to it," Abraham said, his voice husky. "Fuck me, here. Mark me however you want. Don't make me wait, unless you absolutely hate the idea of fucking me."

"Never." Roman growled, fisting a hand in Abraham's hair. He felt very predatory, his coyote closer to the surface than it'd ever been. For one second, he almost pulled himself back, but then Abraham moaned and Roman stopped fighting the wildness taking over.

Still kissing his mate, Roman led him a few steps back from the edge of the slightly raised platform they'd been standing on, over to the soft, thick grass behind it. There, he encouraged Abraham to kneel, and Roman joined him, never breaking the kiss.

When the kiss did end, he pushed Abraham back, helping him to lie down, and lowered himself over Abraham, careful not to lie fully on him.

Abraham parted his lips on a moan. He raised one leg and hooked an ankle around Roman's hips. "God, fuck me, Roman," he begged over and over.

"Going to." He had the lube there behind the platform. Just because he'd never been interested in having sex under the blue moon before didn't mean he hadn't hoped he would tonight. And he did very much want his mate.

To the point that Roman was ravenous for him, couldn't touch or kiss Abraham enough. He rubbed his cock alongside Abraham's as he sucked up a mark on Abraham's neck, right under his jaw.

Roman couldn't grind and mark him enough, couldn't smell or hear him enough. He hungered for Abraham in every way, like an addict needing his fix. And he *did* need Abraham.

Sibilant sounds left Abraham as Roman sucked up another mark after on his warm skin. The salty taste of sweat was mixed with a muskier flavor that was man and beast combined.

Abraham's animal was close to the surface, too. Roman grinned down at him. "Feel it?" He thrust, driving his dick harder against Abraham's. "Feel that animal trying to break out?"

Abraham arched his neck and moaned. "S'that what it is? Holy fuck, it's making me burn so good."

"No, that part's me," Roman asserted before dipping his head and licking Abraham's nipple.

Abraham mewed and wrapped his other leg around Roman's hips, too. "Fuck me, do it, push into me, just push in and—"

Roman scraped his teeth over Abraham's left nipple, seeking to distract him before Roman lost all control and did just what Abraham was begging him to do.

"More, more," Abraham whimpered, giving a full body shudder. "Uhn!" He grabbed a handful of Roman's hair.

Roman rubbed his thumb over the other tit as he began sucking on the first. He worked both nipples into dark, hot peaks that glistened in the moonlight. Roman blew on them, and Abraham jolted, mouth dropping open on a moan.

Then Roman moved down, licking and nibbling his way to Abraham's belly button. He spent a few minutes there, his cock in the grass while Abraham's was burning hot against Roman's chest.

The next moan from Abraham made Roman's dick pulse. The loud, strident hunger in the sounds was obvious.

As much as he'd have liked to spin Abraham around and fuck him hard, Roman didn't. He had enough restraint left to know Abraham wasn't ready yet, even if Abraham didn't seem to realize it.

Roman moved lower and fisted Abraham's shaft. He jacked it a few times, then knelt and pressed his face against the base of it. There, Roman inhaled deeply as he loved to do, and rubbed his nose and cheek against Abraham's groin. He wanted to coat himself in his mate's scent, and he simply enjoyed the feel of Abraham's curly hair against his cheek until he was ready for more.

Once he was, Roman began to lick at one of Abraham's thighs, where it joined to his torso. Roman wanted more room to play, so he pushed at Abraham's legs in silent demand.

As soon as Abraham spread his legs wider, Roman ducked his head and sucked on Abraham's balls.

"Roman, please, let me touch you, too," Abraham begged. "I've never ached like this before!"

Roman nosed Abraham's balls, then nipped at the inside of his thighs before raising his head up and taking the tip of Abraham's cock into his mouth. He glanced up Abraham's long, sexy body, and watched him play with his own nipples for a moment, then Roman licked over Abraham's crown. He pushed his tongue against the slit, wanting to drive Abraham out of his mind.

He had thought he understood how much he needed Abraham before that moment, but no. *That was only the beginning of it. This need for him runs through the very marrow of my bones, into my soul, into every reincarnation of it. We have been, and are, and will be again, mates, always.*

That deep, abiding truth was the moment, the epiphany that Roman hadn't known he'd been waiting for.

The coyote in him howled and yipped, and Roman knew he'd be shifting later, running under the moonlight. He hoped his mate would be with him, shifted as well.

Dwelling on it now was impossible, though. Roman laved Abraham's shaft and took more of that length into his mouth. He fondled Abraham's balls, and stroked his shaft while he bobbed up and down, slowly at first, increasing the speed as his own arousal burned hotter.

Giving head and getting it, Roman didn't know if anal sex could be any better. There was control and freedom in each of the oral positions, and he assumed the same went for anal sex, but sucking Abraham's dick, breaking him apart with pleasure, taking him down deep, drinking his seed while his own jaw ached, the wet, slurping sounds...everything about giving Abraham a blow job was the height of perfection for Roman.

And Abraham made the best sounds when he came, and right before then, and actually throughout the whole thing. Roman loved how Abraham held himself back from thrusting, the way he shivered and his skin pebbled with goosebumps.

Roman couldn't see them then, but he knew they were there.

Abraham whined, the sound a warning that his orgasm was fast approaching. Roman pulled off sucking his cock, kissing the tip as he did so. "Going to fuck you, here, surrounded by our pack. Tell me no if that's not what you want."

"I want it, I want *you*," Abraham said after his first attempt to speak ended in a cough. "Now."

Roman grinned at him. "I like this bossy side of you. Can you feel your animal?"

"Yes, now please —" Abraham cupped his own balls, lifting them up as he spread his legs, exposing his hole to Roman. "Fuck me."

Roman wasn't going to wait any longer. They both wanted the joining. He vaguely heard others fucking and moaning, sounds of pleasure as they had sex. Roman doubted anyone was paying him and Abraham any attention. Sex was thick in the air — the sounds of it, the scent and pheromones.

The lube was right at hand. "Stay on your back." It'd be easier for Abraham, and Roman wanted to see his face.

Abraham hitched his knees up, hooking his left arm under them.

Roman opened the lube, then poured some onto his palm. He closed the tube then set it aside before dipping two fingers in the puddle he held. "Ready?" he asked, pressing his fingertips to Abraham's hot, tight hole.

"More than," Abraham answered.

Roman rubbed, and his fingers sank right into the gripping heat. He pulled them back, thrust them in again. "Going to make you crazy for me."

"Already am." Abraham gulped. "Please, that's plenty. I want to feel your cock stretching me."

Roman twisted his fingers around, pumped them in and out a couple more times, then withdrew them. "I love you," he said as he lined his cock up, his hand shaking on the base of it. "I do."

"I—" Abraham let go of his legs and moaned, eyes rolling, flickering golden yellow in a distinctly *not* human way for just a moment as Roman began to push into him.

He'd thought Abraham's ass felt amazing around his fingers, but that was nothing compared to the way his hole gripped and milked Roman's dick. Roman could hardly breathe as he slowly drove forward, vision hazing even as he tried to clear it, needing to see Abraham's expression clearly. He didn't want to cause him any pain, only pleasure.

Something sizzled and popped to life in Roman's head, a connection he hadn't expected, one that tied him to Abraham even more. He felt Abraham's pleasure, his joy and need, his deep, abiding love for Roman.

And judging by the spark of surprise, Abraham felt Roman's emotions, too.

"Mate," Roman whispered as he bottomed out, his groin pressed to Abraham's ass. "Mine. *Mine!*"

Abraham held him with his left arm, and raised his head for a kiss.

Roman dipped down to give it to him, then pushed himself up on his palms so he could move, pulling back until his cock just stretched Abraham's ring. Gaze locked with his mate's, Roman thrust in, hard, deep.

Abraham grunted, mouth open, fingernails sharp against Roman's back.

Instinct won over. Roman had a bond with Abraham and would know if anything he did was too much. He let go, hips snapping faster and faster against Abraham's buttocks, panting as he dug his knees into the grass for purchase.

Moonlight cast silver light on Abraham's face, and his eyes glowed yellow again. The musky scent of animal was strong between them as they fucked. Roman curled his fingers into the grass, digging under it into the dirt. He thrust harder, whimpering with a need that grew with every deep penetration.

Abraham's ass gripped Roman's cock tighter and tighter. When Abraham let go of him and instead reached down to jack himself off, Roman's eyes nearly crossed at how those sweet inner walls clenched. He lowered himself to his elbows and sealed his mouth to Abraham's in a harsh kiss that hurt and felt perfect at the same time.

Abraham jerked and turned his head aside on a shout.

Roman shoved his cock in as deep as he could and ground his hips against Abraham's buttocks as his climax washed over him in great, all-encompassing waves of ecstasy.

How long it lasted, Roman had no clue. He rode the bliss until his body and spirit realigned. His dick slipped from Abraham's body, and right afterwards, his skin prickled and itched in warning.

"Abraham," he tried to say, but his tongue felt thick and weird, too long. Roman rolled to Abraham's left, vision blurring to the point that he couldn't see anything but a single yellow spot. Pain lanced through his body, then it was gone, and he was him, but he wasn't. Another being was in his head with him, and Roman tipped his head back, nose toward the moon, and he howled.

Something thumped his shoulder.

Roman canted his head, and spied his mate, a glorious shaggy and deadly black bear. Not a grizzly like Gideon, not as large as him, either, but still, nothing to sneer at.

No wonder he didn't fear Miller. Black bears aren't below coyotes on the food chain. And neither did black bears regularly enjoy a coyote for dinner.

Roman yipped at his mate, bouncing, wanting to play.

Abraham grunted, then did something that sounded a lot like a tongue click. He rose up on his hind feet, and flapped his right paw at Roman.

His right paw! Roman noted that it didn't move easily, or as much as the left, but the mobility was more than it had been when Abraham was in human form.

Roman decided running could wait. He wanted to play with Abraham, and see if he'd make more of those clicking noises. Tongue lolling, Roman pounced.

Chapter Eighteen

Abraham woke up on his back, dew coating his skin, and sunlight warming him. He groaned, sore in places he hadn't been aware of in possibly ever, and he slowly sat up.

"Ungh."

He blinked at that sound, and turned his head. He saw Roman beside him, one eye open. "Why'd we sleep on the ground?"

Roman made his unintelligible sound again, then sat up, taking longer than Abraham had to do it. He wiped at his mouth, then rubbed his eyes and yawned. A scratch to his chin and a snort, and Roman seemed to be a little more alert. "Guess a lot of us did."

Abraham looked around then and noticed they were not alone. At least a dozen couples or more were in various stages of waking up in the ceremonial circle.

"So, a black bear. Pretty cool," Roman said. "You don't smell like grizzly."

"Makes me more curious about my genetic parents." Abraham stretched, raising his left arm up, arching until his back popped. His right arm was raised halfway, hovering around at chest level. "What the hell—I knew I could move it more when I shifted, but…" But he didn't know what to say.

Roman's smile could have lit up a city, it was so bright. "That is awesome! See, shifters used to have the ability to heal fast, a lot faster than humans. I think you must have gotten a burst of that power last night."

Abraham was glad for that, but he did wonder. "Does that mean this is as healed as it'll get? It's better than any of the doctors or surgeons or PT folks thought it'd be, but I was hoping for more despite what they all said."

"Give it time," Roman suggested. "We don't know enough to make even an educated guess."

"Okay, I can do that." Abraham lowered both arms. "Still, that *is* a wonderful thing to have happen. I don't know how I'll explain it in the next PT session."

Roman frowned. "Crap. You might need to stop the sessions. We can find someone else, or do some research on our own. Whatever you want to do, I'm with you on it."

Abraham felt the truth of that like a faint echo in his head. "That connection, it was stronger when we were making love."

"It was, but I still feel a hint of what you do, I guess. If I concentrate, I can. If I'm just sitting here, naked, worrying about getting ant bites on my balls, then I don't really feel it," Roman said.

Abraham had leaped up and held his left hand out to Roman. "Get up, for God's sake. I don't want you getting your dangly bits hurt."

Roman laughed and rose to his feet. "That makes two of us."

They gathered up their clothes, damp from the dew, and put them on after shaking each garment out.

Roman picked up the lube and tucked it into his shirt pocket. "Don't want to lose that."

"No, we don't." Abraham wiggled his butt and got a laugh from Roman.

They joined Miller and Gideon at the south curve of the circle. "Need a ride?" Miller asked. "Another bear." He shook his head.

Gideon bounced on his toes. "But I'm still the biggest bear. I tried to get you to play but you were all up in Roman's grill last night."

"All up in his *grill?*" Miller sounded perplexed. "What happened, did you regress into childhood? If so, we're going to have problems."

"Goof," Gideon chided. "You need coffee, and lots of it, to get back to being your cute, charming self."

Abraham could have been wrong, but it sure sounded like Miller mumbled something about someone needing a good spanking soon under his breath.

Well, if that's how they play, more power to them. Abraham held his left hand out to Roman, who held it as they followed Miller and Gideon to the truck. Miller waited until everyone was loaded up in vehicles, then he drove back toward town with the mini-caravan of cars and trucks behind him.

"Want us to take you somewhere other than the motel?" Miller asked. "Breakfast, maybe?"

Abraham left that question to Roman.

"No thanks. We have some food in the mini fridge, and I want to shower. We'll meet y'all at the gallery when it opens," Roman replied.

"Sounds like a plan. We're going to our hotel room, too, then out to rustle up breakfast." Miller let them out, and Abraham and Roman thanked him for the ride. They waved to Gideon, then Abraham panicked for a moment until Roman dug the key card for their room out of his shirt pocket.

"I at least had enough sense to keep the pocket snapped shut, surprisingly," Roman said. He unlocked the door and opened it, then went very still.

Abraham acted on instinct, pushing himself in front of Roman, reaching for a weapon he no longer had strapped to his hip, and with a hand that couldn't have gripped it anyway.

He smelled a scent that was wrong, not his or Roman's, not a friend's. There was a bitter, sharp scent lingering in the room that might have singed a few of his nose hairs.

And it looked like their clothes had been ripped to shreds. The bedding was stripped off and torn, the mattress rancid with something on it that Abraham didn't want to examine too closely.

He started to back away, whispering, "I don't think they're still in the room, but ease back."

Roman slipped one hand into the waistband of Abraham's pants and pulled.

Abraham had no intention of sending Roman away and going into the room. He moved with Roman, closing the door quietly. Once clear of it, Abraham turned around and had only a split second to register the Tahoe in the street and the barrel of the rifle pointing out of it.

"Down!" he shouted, diving at Roman.

Fear or instinct, whatever it was, took over, and Abraham shifted before they hit the ground. Roman landed in coyote form, and he bolted for the SUV.

Abraham roared, lumbering after his mate as a bullet zipped past him. He couldn't run, couldn't get his right paw and arm to work as it should. He reared up on his back paws and roared again, hoping to keep the shooter's attention, and *now* the scent back in the hotel room registered. It was the same as the one in his apartment in El Paso, but he hadn't been able to make that connection until just then.

Roman tucked his body low to the ground but kept running for the truck. People came out into the streets, and Abraham couldn't worry over what they might have seen. He hoped no humans had spotted him and Roman shifting, but surviving this attack, and keeping his mate alive, took priority over that concern.

To that end, Abraham bellowed again, slapping the air with his left paw. *Me, me! Look at me, you fucking Vonheimer! What the hell is your people's problem?*

Abraham dropped down to three paws and started toward the Tahoe again. It was his Tahoe, which didn't bode well for Duff, and implied, at least to Abraham, that the apartment fire hadn't been an act of nature.

Roman spun to the right in a quick move. Abraham saw another coyote and a big grizzly came running from the hotel a block down. They were followed by more animals.

He kept heading for the Tahoe, saw Vonheimer move the rifle just an inch or so, and knew what was about to happen. He just hoped it didn't kill him, or maim him too badly, when the bullet hit him.

Abraham tucked his head down and expected to feel the agonizing pain of being shot. Instead, he heard Roman growl, then the scrape of metal and claws had him raising his head. The rifle went off, and Abraham screamed — roared, rather, but Roman wasn't hurt. He had the rifle in his muzzle and dropped it just as Vonheimer sped away.

Miller barked and growled as he went racing after the Tahoe. Sirens wailed, and the racket that caused — coyotes howling at the top of their lungs—was headache-inducing.

The police car came flying down the road, and Miller spun off to the shoulder, getting out of the way. He ran back to parking lot of the Motel 6, then snapped his muzzle, long canines bared, before turning and loping toward the gallery.

Abraham and Roman nosed each other, checking for injuries. They were unharmed. With that assurance made, they went to the gallery with the other pack members.

Miller shifted quickly and strode to his office. He returned wearing sweats and a long sleeved T-shirt. "This is fucking enough!" He slapped his fist right hand against the palm of his left. "I have *had it* with these bastards attacking my pack, my town! They came here and hurt Roman, and because some of them were made to pay for it, they think they have a right to be pissed off, to make us pay for protecting our own, for what? I don't *fucking care anymore!* Get somewhere safe, or get ready to go out with me and Gid. This shit ends, now."

Not a one of them left the gallery.

Miller looked at them, starting with Roman. "Are you sure? None of you are obligated." His gaze went to Abraham next.

Abraham growled. He wasn't obligated, no, but he had vowed to protect Roman long before they'd become mates. That wasn't about to change.

After checking with everyone, Miller started handing out orders. "Rudy, you, Miranda, Kyra and Paul, shift. Go get your trucks. We need the beds on them to haul everyone."

The doors to the gallery swung open, the bell chiming. In walked Jess, and a handsome man holding two rifles, one in each hand. He had a hip holster as well, with a three-fifty-seven in it.

"We're here to help," Jack said. He'd been at the ceremony the night before, but as a human, hadn't shifted. "And I brought reinforcements."

Jess moved aside. Jack's Hummer had a wicked-looking gun mounted beside the sunroof. "It's even legal. I have a special permit," Jack said.

Abraham wasn't about to argue with him.

"Good. Can you take a couple of people with you?" Miller asked.

"Of course. Someone needs to work that gun or drive while I shoot it." Jack gestured to the Hummer. "Whoever's riding with us, come on."

Abraham and Roman waited to ride in the truck bed with Miller and Gideon, as well as the three of the Fervent Five. The other two, Kyra and Paul, were driving.

It was a tight fit, but manageable since they'd all returned to human form. Someone had fetched clothing—sweats and tops for everyone—so they didn't have to ride back there naked. Or as their animals, which would have caused problems if humans spotted them.

Like they probably had in the motel parking lot. Abraham was betting on Miller being able to spin it into a theory about the tornado messing with the wildlife. He'd be sure to suggest it to Miller in case the idea hadn't occurred to him yet. It was Abraham's experience that people saw so much weird shit online and on TV now days that nothing much fazed them.

He hoped his theory would hold up in Del Rey.

"Iker called in with his location," Miller had said before they left. "He wasn't on duty when he went after

Vonheimer earlier, and he doesn't think anyone has called it in or asked for reinforcements."

That sounded like an all-clear to hunt down and kill Gentry Vonheimer, and while Abraham wanted his mate safe, vengeance and vigilantism was wrong. If he had to, he'd intervene to keep anyone from committing murder.

But if Vonheimer was trying to kill *them*, self-defense was an acceptable action to take.

The ride was bumpy once they left the main road outside of Del Rey. "Miller, what are we doing?" Abraham asked, just for clarification.

Miller rubbed his chin. "Well, as much as I'd like to make sure this is over for good, I can't sanction murdering anyone, if that's what you're worried about. I won't hesitate to kill in self-defense or defense of my mate, or pack, either. I don't want to do that, but I will before I let someone I care about get hurt."

"Okay." Abraham glanced at Roman, then back at Miller. "Maybe that's something you should have said in the gallery. It kind of sounded like the plan was to find Vonheimer and annihilate him."

Miller nodded. "I'll make sure everyone understands not to do that." His mouth kicked up in a lopsided grin. "Especially Jack. The hell kind of survivalist is he with that big gun on his Hummer?"

"Maybe it's for fighting zombies," Tandy suggested. "I've seen vehicles armed for a zombie apocalypse."

"He *does* watch that TV show," Miller said. "Mom's into it now, too. I think I'd rather him just have the gun because it makes him feel manly than for him to believe in the possibility of zombies."

"Like it's so far-fetched." Gideon waved one hand. "Hello! Shifters are real. So are space aliens. Don't rule out living dead people with a craving for braaaaaiiiinnns."

Miller huffed and shook his head. "Aliens aren't real." His crooked grin turned into a full laugh.

Abraham felt better about this mission, as he decided to call it. No one was screaming for Vonheimer's head on a plate.

"Are you okay?" he asked Roman.

Roman nodded. "Sure. Are you?"

Abraham didn't press. "I'm fine. Glad you are too." He kissed Roman, and nearly busted both their lips when the tuck hit a bump.

"Smooth," Gideon said. "Real smooth. Bloody lips are so not sexy."

Roman flipped Gideon off.

Kyra turned and the road became bumpier.

"Shouldn't be much further. He's past the ceremonial hall, at the ruins five miles out." Miller checked his phone. "Iker's holding him off, but he thinks Duff might be in the Tahoe. He can't be sure."

Abraham asked, "Where's Gael?"

"He had an appointment this morning in El Paso at a homeless shelter, so he'd left early," Miller explained. "I left it to Iker to either tell him what's going on or not."

"If he doesn't, Gael will be pissed off." Gideon yelped as the truck hit a dip. "Jeez, my butt's already sore!"

"Nice going," Miller groused when Abraham and several others looked at him. "Don't look at me. We weren't the only ones fucking last night."

Kyra turned again, then she brought the truck to a stop.

"Close as we're gonna get in the truck right now. Shift time." Miller stood up and began to strip.

Abraham debated whether or not to shift. With his right arm and hand still not much use, he couldn't shoot a gun, but in bear form, running on all fours was a challenge. He really had to hobble on three.

Roman touched his hand. "I'll stay with you, in whatever form you want."

"Yeah, y'all don't have to shift, and you don't have to come with us, even. I'm gonna have us spread out and try to circle around, get behind Vonheimer. Paul's taking the other truck farther down a few miles." Miller leaped from the truck bed. "Ain't wrong to hang back, ain't wrong not to."

"We'll come," Abraham decided, checking with Roman.

"Yes." Roman stood up. "In what form?"

Abraham stood as well. "I think I'm going to start out just like this, but you can shift if you want to. Might be a good idea, actually, if you can scent better as a coyote."

Roman took his clothes off while Miller went over his plan in greater detail.

"Questions?" Miller asked.

All he received was a round of 'no's.

"All right then. I just got the texts from Paul, and Jack. We're heading out in two minutes." He shifted, and everyone but Abraham followed their alpha into their animal form.

Two minutes seemed to drag by, then Miller put his nose up and he sniffed. He gave a soft yip, lowered his head, and started off at a lope.

Roman and Abraham moved slower. They veered to the right, taking the shortest part of the planned trail. Miller and Gideon, along with Jack, Jess, Lilith and Rudy, would be forming the back part of the circle around Vonheimer. They hoped to be able to draw his attention and disarm him.

It sounded easy, though Abraham knew better. He could only hope none of the pack members were hurt or killed, before it was all said and done.

Roman remembered when even thinking about any of the men who'd violated him would strike terror in his heart. That was no longer the case—he hated them, and hated what they'd done to the flirtatious, innocent boy he'd been, but he did *not* fear them. It was liberating, and released him too from the desire to see them all dead. He'd had understandably vicious fantasies of revenge, but now understood that justice and revenge were two different things, and only one of those wouldn't erode a person's soul.

Walking beside Abraham, Roman wished this whole thing was over with already. He just wanted his loved ones safe, and he prayed this would be the last time they had to face the twisted men who'd caused so much pain and chaos.

He kept sniffing and listened for any sounds that were out of place. Nothing alarmed him. He and Abraham made it to their stopping point, a large boulder to the west of where the Tahoe was parked about half a mile away.

Iker's police car was a quarter mile to the south of that. Iker was on one knee beside it, using the vehicle for cover.

A shot rang out, and Iker returned fire.

"Damn it, Iker's out there alone." Abraham cursed again. "Sitting here doing nothing while a fellow law enforcement officer is being fired upon is wrong!"

Roman shifted and stood up, pressing close to Abraham. "It can't be helped. He's got the strength of the pack—and Jack's insanely big gun—surrounding him."

"Right," Abraham said, almost snapping the word out. "And let's hope Jack or someone else doesn't shoot in Iker's direction and kill him."

Roman hadn't thought of that. "No, no that can't happen." He peered around the boulder at Iker. "He's going to move." He'd have to if anyone behind Vonheimer was going to shoot and not risk hitting him. "Isn't he?"

Abraham closed his eyes for about ten seconds then opened them. "Have faith. We need to have faith."

Roman shivered. "That's what the old prophecy said. When we were trying to figure out why we'd lost our shifter everything. We'd lost our faith."

"And now we need it again." Abraham squatted, Roman crouching with him. "How do we do that, Roman? What does a medicine man do in times when faith is needed most?"

Roman slipped his hands into Abraham's. "We pray, and chant, and meditate. We will the world to do this one thing, to keep our pack mate safe, all of our pack members safe. We try, in the way we try best, to help."

Abraham gave his hands a squeeze. "Then that's what we'll do."

Roman pulled Abraham back up. "And we don't crouch down, hide behind a rock."

"What do you mean?" Abraham's voice had threads of panic in it. "We have to stay hidden."

Roman took a step back. "We have to *have faith.*"

"Wait. There's faith, then there's—" Abraham broke off. "No, no, I won't doubt you. I won't."

Roman wasn't doubting himself either. He moved further out, raised their joined hands up to the sky and began to chant words he'd never spoken or read before.

He opened his heart and mind, and reached for that source of life and light he'd learned existed. When he'd been younger, he'd been an atheist, and he'd been angry about it. He knew that wasn't how every atheist was, but he'd had to be mad. He'd had to rail and hate and scream to survive.

Now, he believed in the spirits that had always been, in the power that regenerated itself second by second, breath by breath, heartbeat by heartbeat.

It was that belief, that faith, that flowed through him and into Abraham, from Abraham, who chanted every word with him, back into Roman. They had a circuit of power and protection arcing out from where they stood. Roman saw nothing but that brightness, the pure and good energy pulled in from the universe, pouring back out into it.

Then he stopped chanting, and Abraham's voice was silenced as well. Roman gestured outward with their joined hands, sending that protective sphere out to his pack mates.

He saw Iker shift and run, paws slapping the ground as he moved faster than should have been possible, reaching a copse of trees as Vonheimer shot at hm.

Roman could pinpoint exactly where Vonheimer, and someone who was a relative of some sort—they shared the exact same auras—were hidden amongst the ruins. And he saw Duff's form in the back of the Tahoe, so still, his life force hovering just under the skin, a sign that he wasn't far from death.

Roman could only hold on, beg Duff to hold on, and send out the positive energy cycling through him and Abraham.

"Drop your weapons," Jack boomed. "We've got you surrounded, and you're not—"

A barrage of gunfire cut him off, and the returning gunfire put out the aura of the Vonheimers once and for all.

Epilogue

"I'm going to start digging and seeing if I can learn anything about my family history." Abraham sat down beside Roman in their temporary dwelling, a portable tiny home that was cute but too small. Roman's books would have filled it up. "I want to know where I came from."

"We can do some things ourselves, some spirit walks, if you want. I don't know what we'd learn, but it's possible to go back in time, and to travel to other places." Roman blushed. "I know that sounds crazy, but I believe it."

"Doesn't sound crazy." Abraham wouldn't doubt anything Roman told him after the showdown last week out by the ruins. He'd felt so much pure, good energy flowing through them that he'd never doubt its existence. "What happened to us, that energy was ancient, eternal, I mean. It always has been, always will be. Like us."

"Like us," Roman agreed. "You know, if we can learn how to send our spirits through time, we can't just do it for shits and giggles."

"No, that'd be contrary to the positive energy," Abraham agreed. "We'll see what we can find out through other means first. Which means, you and I have a dinner meeting with my parents next Sunday."

Roman sat up straighter. "What? When did this happen? I thought y'all didn't talk or get along."

"Dinner," Abraham drawled. "With my parents, next Sunday. It happened when they finally returned my call while you were in the bathroom. We don't talk, obviously, or get along. They hate that I have the big inheritance, but if they'll talk to me about what I want to know, I'll be looser with it."

Roman's anger brought a smoky scent to the room. "You shouldn't have to bribe them or pay for them to share what they know about your past."

"It is what it is," Abraham said. "I doubt they know anything about my past directly, but if they know some things about my grandmother's husband, that might give me a direction to start looking. I've tried to find his death certificate with no luck. It seems to have just been wiped out of databases."

"That's weird. Do you think your grandmother had it erased, or what? What's your best guess?" Roman asked.

"I'd go with that one. If he died in a way that was potentially embarrassing or unbelievable, or even insulting to his perceived masculinity, she might have had his death certificate destroyed somehow. Money's a powerful thing," Abraham added.

"But not the most powerful thing. That'd be love." Roman tossed his blond hair back, doing his favorite 'hair flip' move.

It was sexy as hell. Abraham's dick began to harden. "We have time to research her, and anyone else involved. We still need to meet with my parents for dinner Sunday."

"If you insist." Roman twirled a few strands of hair around his fingers. "So what should we do now? It's dark out, we've visited Duff, Gael and Iker, had dinner, a shower, and there's nothing on TV. I guess we could play cards."

"Play cards." Abraham pretended to think it over. "I suppose we could. Rummy, maybe? Gin or regular? Oh! Strip poker?"

"Now you're talking," Roman said. "I'll get the deck, except let's minus the card playing and just get naked."

Abraham stood up. "In this small home, we've already had sex on every surface."

"Yes, but you haven't made love to me, not in every way yet, so we have to start over and break in every surface again." Roman fluttered his lashes at Abraham.

Abraham's mouth had gone dry, and he had to take a sip of his water before he could speak. "Are you saying what I think you're saying?"

Roman laughed. "Why are we talking around it? I want your dick in my ass. Is that plain enough?"

Most of Abraham's blood apparently rushed to his cock. He stared at Roman then nodded.

"I'll get the lube." Roman leaned back and plucked it off the shelf. "When we move into our new home, once it's built, we'll have to keep a few bottles of lube in every room. I like not having to get up and hunt for it." He opened the bottle then handed it to Abraham.

He set the bottle down on the table, and stood up. Over the past week, he'd gained even more use of his right arm and hand, and his shoulder along with the rest of the injured parts hurt a lot less. It made taking off his shirt easier, and sliding his pants down a breeze.

Abraham had himself bared and his hard cock in hand, but his thoughts scattered as Roman began to undress as if he were stripping to music.

Hips swaying seductively, Roman began to hum while slowly raising his shirt up, exposing his pale stomach inch by tantalizing inch. He turned his back to Abraham and moved his butt, not in a ribald way, just rocking it from side to side.

More skin was bared, the long line of his spine appearing as Roman raised the shirt higher. When Roman stretched his arms up, his ribs were displayed, then he spun around and tossed the shirt right at Abraham, giggling as he flung it.

Abraham caught it and pressed it to his nose, his gaze locked with Roman's as he inhaled deeply, taking in his mate's scent.

"Oh, that's making my cock even harder," Roman murmured. "Turns me on that you like the way I smell."

"Love it," Abraham corrected. He rubbed the material against his cheeks.

"Even better." Roman winked at him, then began working the buttons of his jeans open. "And am I going commando tonight, or not?"

"If you aren't, you'll be out of your underwear soon," Abraham vowed.

Roman laughed and let his pants fall to the floor. He had nothing else on. "Easy access. That's how we both like it." He fisted his dick loosely. "Mm. Feels good. See how hard I am? That's because I want you to fuck me. To make love to me. To bend me over the table and have your way with me. Except, I'm not going to be passive."

Abraham moved away from the table, which wasn't very far from it, considering the space available. "Of course you're not. Tell me what you want." He was nervous and trying not to babble.

Roman smiled brightly. He didn't appear to be suffering from any of the nerves Abraham was. "I want you to rim me until I'm begging you to fuck me, then I want you to put that very nice cock of yours right here." He patted his butt. "And you can start it all off by kissing me senseless."

Abraham held out his hand to Roman. "Think I'm already on the senseless part myself."

Roman clenched his ass in anticipation. He'd been thinking about this for a long time. If he were honest — and he was — his first fantasy about having Abraham fuck him had been a few weeks after first meeting him. Now, he was finally getting that wish.

He stopped in front of Abraham. "That kiss?" His dick brushed against Abraham's stomach as he went up onto his toes to meet Abraham halfway.

Abraham parted his lips just in time for Roman to press his against them. Roman kissed him with all the hunger and need, all the love and faith and hope he had in him. He ached for Abraham in a way that, a year ago, he'd never have believed possible. He'd thought sexual attraction would always be for other people, and he wouldn't even miss it. Then he'd met Ranger Abraham Evans, and Roman had found it necessary to examine himself and his desires more closely.

And he'd had to make the decision to heal. Until then, he'd never understood that he had to work actively toward that goal. Now he wanted nothing more than to find out what it felt like to let go and give himself to his mate in this new way. If it wasn't as good as blow jobs, or as good as topping Abraham, then Roman would skip it after this time.

But he had a feeling it was going to be a very good experience.

Abraham caressed him from shoulders to the top of his buttocks, up again, then down as they kissed. Roman wanted those big hands to go lower, to cup his ass, to knead it and part his cheeks.

He tilted his head back. He needed to ask for what he wanted, so he would. Or he'd demand it. "Abraham, touch me. My ass, touch my ass."

Abraham kissed him again and finally brought his hands down, cupping Roman's ass gently at first, holding each cheek as if it were fragile.

Roman growled. "Abraham, don't treat me like I'm going to break."

"I wouldn't dream of it. Your skin's just so soft here." Then Abraham squeezed, and Roman gasped, amazed at how such a thing could make him tingle from his butthole to the tip of his dick.

"Good?" Abraham squeezed again.

"So good," Roman said. "More?"

Abraham kissed him and kneaded his cheeks for several minutes, then he startled Roman by goosing him.

"Hey!" Roman squealed with laughter. "That's not sexy!"

"It made you laugh, which is very sexy," Abraham countered. "I would prefer we move to the bed, unless you're insistent on the table. It's hard on the back, though, and it'd be your back on it." He traced the length of Roman's spine.

"Bed, then." Roman turned in his arms, and rubbed his backside against Abraham's leg. "Hurry though."

It was only a half dozen steps to the bed. Roman tumbled down eagerly and Abraham joined him, stretching out on his side, reaching for Roman.

Another kiss, then Abraham had him on his back and was kissing Roman's collarbone.

Roman hadn't known he could make that particularly lusty sound, but apparently he had more sex-yum noises than he'd thought.

Roman rested his hands in Abraham's hair and let Abraham have his way, let him kiss and love on him, his lips, his neck, his chest.

Abraham's slow, sexy foreplay ratcheted Roman's need up to higher levels with each passing minute.

"You like this?" Abraham asked, gently scraping his teeth over Roman's left nipple.

"Fuck yeah," Roman gasped out, holding Abraham's head there. "Don't stop."

"Won't," Abraham responded, then he proceeded to make Roman burn with arousal.

He worked both of Roman's nipples over until he could feel every heartbeat in them. Roman couldn't be still, couldn't stop thrusting and whining and wanting.

Abraham reached down and touched the tip of Roman's shaft. Roman almost came on the spot.

"I like that reaction." Abraham sat up then straddled Roman's waist. "I want to kiss every inch of you. Don't think I'd last through it. Look at what just kissing you and touching your dick has done to me." He held his cock out. "All wet-tipped and so hard I could use it for a bat—not that I'm so inclined."

"Good. I wouldn't want you to hurt that gorgeous dick," Roman replied. "But I would like to feel it in my ass sometime tonight."

Abraham moved back down to kneel between Roman's legs. "Well, if you're going to insist..." He cupped Roman's butt cheeks then squeezed them firmly.

"Yess," Roman hissed, wanting more than just that. "It's not enough."

"No it isn't." Abraham traced the seam of his crack.

Licks of bliss shot out from the simple touch. Roman arched his back and spread his knees further apart. "My hole, touch me there. Get…finger or tongue, just something, please."

"Touch you like this?" Abraham pressed one fingertip to his pucker. "Gently massage it?"

"Argh!" The light touch very nearly rocketed Roman into orgasm. If he wasn't careful, he'd come before he ever got fucked, and that would be an entirely not fun kind of getting fucked!

"More?" Abraham pressed harder. "Not without the lube, which I left on the table."

"Abraham," Roman wailed. "Get it!"

"On my way." Abraham got up and was back in less time than it would have taken Roman to protest. He set the tube on the bed. "I hate the taste of lube. It's so chemical-y."

"Then don't—" Roman yelped as Abraham flipped him over.

"This way." Abraham had him bent over the side of the bed in seconds. "Yeah, open that pretty ass up for me."

Roman reached back and parted his cheeks.

"Sweet man. Sweet, sweet man." Then Abraham licked him, right over his hole.

Roman's world changed for the better then. He'd not been rimmed before, and he'd missed out on something he could have been enjoying receiving as well as he enjoyed giving it. He was learning that when it came to sex with his mate, everything that felt good to do to Abraham also felt pretty damn amazing to have done to himself. He'd remember that.

Abraham cupped Roman's balls and pressed his tongue more insistently against Roman's hole.

Roman felt the muscle relax and give way, followed by the warm, slick glide of Abraham's tongue penetrating him.

It was too much, yet nowhere near enough, and Abraham kept at it — licking, fucking, kissing his hole until Roman was ready to sob for more.

Roman pleaded with his mate instead. "P-please, Abraham. I need you."

"I'm right here," Abraham said. "Right here, worshiping you, loving you. Can't get enough of you, of the sounds you make, the taste—" He pushed his tongue into Roman's ass again, then withdrew it. "Back up on the bed."

"How?"

"Butt up, shoulders down, and give me room to move behind you," Abraham instructed.

Roman clambered onto the bed and drew his legs up under his chest. "Tell me you'll be fucking me soon. Making love to me. Tell me that."

"I'll be making love to you soon." Abraham got on the bed behind him. "After I rim you some more."

And rimming Roman more was exactly what Abraham did just as soon as Roman had rolled onto his belly. Abraham tongued Roman's hole open, laved it repeatedly, left it wet and slick and ready for more.

While he drove Roman to new heights with his talented mouth and tongue, Abraham also fondled Roman's balls again, occasionally slipping his hand down past them to stroke Roman's dick.

Roman rolled his head from side to side, moaning and calling out Abraham's name. It felt so good, having Abraham rim him, but at the same time, he wanted

Abraham's cock in him. That would have required a level of flexibility that Roman couldn't even imagine.

"Abraham, now," Roman urged finally, when he was close to coming. "Now, or I'll come soon, and you won't be able to touch my ass or dick until I'm not so sensitive."

"Can't have that." Abraham kissed him right at the top of his crack. "I need the lube. There it is."

Roman moved over onto his back, and watched Abraham open the tube then slick his fingers and cock with lube. "Next time, I want to put that on your dick. I love it, but especially when it's slippery and glistening. Yum."

"Next time you can pour lube over my entire body. You can do whatever you want with me, at any time." Abraham wiggled his fingers. "Including telling me to put these in my ass and have me stretch myself for your cock."

That was a beautiful idea but not what Roman wanted. "I'm beginning to think you don't want me like this."

"Impossible," Abraham scoffed. "I want you in every way. I was just throwing out a fantasy of mine. I think fingering myself for you would be a lot of fun, and sexy."

"It would, later. Right now, the sexiest thing in the world would be your cock in my ass." To that end, he sat up, then got onto his hands and knees, hoping the temptation would speed Abraham up. Roman wiggled his backside at his mate. "Soon."

"Your wish and all." Abraham didn't tease him anymore. "And mine." He pushed one lubed finger slowly into Roman's ass. "Ungh, you're so tight, it's going to take forever to work you open."

"Then do it. You can go faster. That feels really, really good." Roman arched his back. "Oh, oh yes, right there." That had to be his prostate, and the pleasure zinging out from it when Abraham touched it was going to send Roman over the edge. "Maybe back off it before I come?"

Abraham kissed Roman's back. "I know how you feel. So close, and frustrated, but incredible, and wanting more, but wanting to come. Oh, I am, believe me. Just"—he pulled his finger out—"gotta keep"— and thrust it back in—"doing this."

Roman moaned and began to move, rocking back and forth, clenching his inner muscles so that they gripped and loosened in time with Abraham's thrusts and withdrawals.

Abraham kept stroking him, stimulating Roman more with every penetration. "Do you know how hard it is, trying not whimper at the thought of your ass all hot and slick around my cock? Can't do it. Can't not let you know how sexy you are, how tight and perfect your ass is. And I'm going to open you up more, get a second finger in, because if I don't, I'm going to just come from doing this, and that'd be embarrassing," Abraham continued. "But I think I could. Could climax because watching this—" He slid both digits into Roman. "This is the sexiest sight, ever." He found Roman's prostate and caressed it.

Roman managed to look over his shoulder at Abraham, needing to see him. "More," he begged before lowering his head to his forearms.

"Hm, that look on your face might even be sexier. You are, without a doubt, the sexiest person in existence," Abraham continued. "And you are mine, all mine, inside and out, heart and soul and body."

"And you're mine just the same," Roman managed to say before Abraham touched his prostate again. Then Roman could only mewl like a hungry kitten as pleasure warmed him deep inside.

"Third one," Abraham whispered in a reverent tone. "Going to watch your hole stretch around them all. Tell you how it looks, thinning as I push them further in, the skin goes from purple to almost lavender."

Roman wanted to scream for him to go faster, but the burn and ache to his ring kept him from making a stupid demand. He could, however, talk like Abraham was, give him some verbal descriptions.

"It feels so good, the fullness, the movement," Roman said. "Just when I think I know which I like best, in or out, I change my mind. I think I just like having a part of you in me, period."

"Yeah, and I'm not doing this right if you're still so coherent." Abraham began to move his fingers faster, and with greater force. "I'm watching my fingers slide in and out, in and out. Your hole is glistening with lube. Someday I'd love for you to do this to me, but not stop. Put your hand in me, and fist me, slow, slow, until I couldn't take it anymore and I came."

"You're killing me." Roman whimpered. "I want to do that. I want to feel your heat around my hand, my wrist." Anything else he'd been planning to say was forgotten as Abraham gave his prostate some more loving.

Roman got a hand on his own cock and squeezed hard to try to curb his orgasm before it could hit. *No coming, no coming until he's got that gorgeous cock in me and is fucking me through this mattress.*

"Are you ready? I think you are, but you tell me." Abraham kept his fingers in Roman, but didn't move them.

"I am so ready," Roman answered after clearing his throat twice. "Make love to me now."

"Now," Abraham agreed. "Now I'm going make us both lose it. I hope I can last long enough to get a full stroke in."

"You'd better," Roman teased. "Otherwise I might cry." And he might not be joking after all.

"That'd make two of us. I plan to enjoy your tight ass for as long as I can hold out." Abraham took his fingers out and wiped them on a cloth beside the bed. Then he got into position behind Roman again. "Promise you won't push back. Trust me to do this."

"Of course I trust you. I do." Roman arched his lower back. "Now please, hurry up. I might lose it and start screaming if you don't."

"I don't mind if you give me screams of pleasure, but if it's anything else, a scream will probably put an end to my erection." Abraham lined up his dick. "And no more talk from me about that." He prodded at Roman's hole. "Breath, push out, and trust me."

"I do, I swear." Roman followed the rest of Abraham's directions.

"Yeah," Abraham rasped as he started pushing harder. "You've got the tightest ass, such a perfect bubble."

Roman pushed out again, and Abraham loosed a string of curse words. That loss of control helped Roman to regain his own, at least a little. "Mmm, yeah, keep it coming, honey. Give me all of your dick."

"I'm trying, but you're so tight, and I want to let go and thrust and thrust and—I won't. I'm taking it slow, enjoying it." Abraham gave his ass a squeeze. "Almost all the way in, just a few more inches."

Rather than continuing forward, Abraham pulled out almost completely. Before Roman could ask what he was doing, Abraham began pushing into him again.

Abraham did this over and over, filling Roman almost to the hilt, then pulling back.

Roman began to caress his own shaft, timing his movements to match those of Abraham's thrusts.

"Ready for more?" Abraham asked. "All of me?"

"Yeah." Roman couldn't get anything else past his dry throat.

Abraham rocked forward, and this time didn't stop until his groin was pressed against Roman's ass.

Roman moved his hips, seeing how it felt to have such a large dick deep inside him. He liked it—no, he loved it, loved his mate.

"Keep moving and I'm going to have to move, too," Abraham warned.

Roman tried to say, "Okay," but it came out more like a blend of consonants without a single vowel.

Abraham must have understood him anyway. Abraham began to withdraw, then thrust in, slow and not so hard at first, but his hips snapped faster with each return of his cock to Roman's ass.

Roman found his voice when need pounded in his veins. "Give me more!"

"Gonna give you more." Abraham grabbed him by the hips and let loose, pulling back until the rim of his cockhead stretched Roman's hole, then shoving in fast and hard.

Roman slammed back with complete lack of inhibition. He wanted Abraham to pound him over and over, and he couldn't speak to get that request out, but he could show Abraham.

Abraham curled over him and fucked him even harder. "So… So good."

Roman would have agreed had he been able. He was being fucked senseless, though, and it seemed that senseless was indeed occurring.

Until Abraham stopped, those wonderful thrusts gone without explanation—although not for long. He tapped Roman's butt. "Turn over onto your back?"

Roman complied quickly. He started to pull his legs up, but Abraham stopped him. "Around me, unless you really want your knees up by your ears."

"Next time," Roman scraped out. He wound his legs around his mate, and when Abraham had his cock in place, Roman tightened his legs. "In, in!"

Abraham thrust, breaching Roman again, spreading him, making his hole burn and clench.

"Fuck, want to...to kiss you," Abraham got out in between strokes.

Roman wanted that too.

Abraham must have seen it in his eyes. He bent and kissed Roman, tongue plunging deep like his cock, then sat up and started a fast, powerful rhythm that had his balls slapping Roman's ass.

Roman pinched one of his nipples, then reached up and pinched one of Abraham's.

"Ro—" Abraham slammed into him. "Oh, I—I—"

The wild look in his was an addictive sight to see. Roman squeezed his ass and jacked his dick while Abraham started to come apart, eyes glazing over before he bowed his head and let go.

And he took Roman with him, the two of them climaxing at the same time, Abraham's cum spurting into him while Roman's seed shot out onto his stomach and the bed.

Roman almost curled into a fetal position as his orgasm rippled through him in waves. He felt Abraham drop down over him, heard the long, deep moan, felt the warmth of Abraham's breath over his forehead.

Slowly, Roman became cognizant of more things, like the cramp in his left calf and the cooling mess on his stomach. His mouth was dry still, and he needed a glass of water before he possibly keeled over from dehydration.

"You fucked the strength right outta me," he said after another minute or three. "Can't move."

Abraham chuckled and got off of him. "My legs feel like gelatin. Smooshy."

"Smooshy." Roman liked it. "That's a good word, and an apt description. Unfortunately, I'm smooshy and need water before my throat becomes the Sahara."

"I'll get it, and a washcloth for you." Abraham kissed the tip of his nose, then got up. "Want anything else?"

"No, just water, and you." Roman had everything he needed, everything he wanted. He couldn't have dreamed of a better life, and he never would have been able to imagine someone like Abraham—so kind, fun and giving, and a bear—would be his mate.

It was funny how life could change, how fate stepped in sometimes, and how love could heal a battered heart.

Someday, he and Abraham would have children, a mix of bears and coyotes, and they'd tell their children of the struggles and pain life could hand a person, and all the beauty and love that could make a heart whole again.

About the Author

A native Texan, Bailey spends her days spinning stories around in her head, which has contributed to more than one incident of tripping over her own feet. Evenings are reserved for pounding away at the keyboard, as are early morning hours. Sleep? Doesn't happen much. Writing is too much fun, and there are too many characters bouncing about, tapping on Bailey's brain demanding to be let out.

Caffeine and chocolate are permanent fixtures in Bailey's office and are never far from hand at any given time. Removing either of those necessities from Bailey's presence can result in what is known as A Very, Very Scary Bailey and is not advised under any circumstances.

Bailey loves to hear from readers. You can find her contact information, website details and author profile page at http://www.pride-publishing.com.

Made in the USA
San Bernardino, CA
18 February 2016